SHE WANNA HOOD N*GGA

NIDDA

Visit Our Website To Sign-up For Our Mailing List
www.UrbanChaptersPublications.com
**If you would like to join our team, submit the first 3-4
chapters of your completed manuscript to**
Submissions@UrbanChapterspublications.com

A NOTE FROM THE AUTHOR

I listen to all feedback good and bad. I take that with me to Microsoft word every time I open it. I was asked why didn't I write about regular hood guys who didn't have the keys to the street handed to them? Why did all my male characters have to be 6'4 and buff? Why can't I talk about regular females that aren't built like the models on magazines, so with this novella, I am delivering what was requested.

You have heard about Shnikia and Sevino in Married to a Boss sleeping with a Savage and Knocked Down by Love & Picked up by a Dope boy if you read those. If you haven't, go ahead and read them, but you don't have to in order to read this. This story is about two sworn enemies being pulled together by love, even in the midst of a war.

This novella is dedicated to Joyce Ann. From the first time that I met you, you were real af and the most brutally honest person I've ever met. You welcomed me to Colorado when other people didn't. You didn't care what you said and how nobody felt about it. In the short time I knew you, you definitely taught me not to hold my tongue for nobody! You were taken too soon and will be missed.

1

SHNIKIA RICHARDSON

"I'm ready to go. You ready?" My best friend, Black, asked.

"Let's just stay a little longer," I whispered because I know when we leave here, my boyfriend Rayvon is goin' to be ready to get back to the block. If my brother Bloccc had it his way, he would have never left. It's our senior prom, and I want to have these memories because next week me and Black will be finally done with high school. She's going to be doing what she does best: hair, and I'm going to be taking my state test soon to be a CNA. I also will be starting at Denver Community College in the fall. Then I plan to transfer to Denver University to complete my nursing degree.

Black had an attitude since we picked her up. She didn't want to come because her and her dude, Mike are trippin' right now. I didn't think that he would go that far to not come to prom, but he did. I had Rayvon calling him last night to talk him into coming, but he was persistent that it wasn't going to happen. Black looks beautiful in her dress; Black is always all the way together and tonight is no different. She has pretty smooth, black skin, big, dark brown eyes, and a perfect shape. She'll stay up all night doing heads to stay in the latest of everything. Everybody be tryin' to get at Black. Even my brother Trigga stays pressin' her.

"Come on," I said, pulling Rayvon up from his chair as he answered his phone.

"Wassup?" Rayvon said as he followed me to the dance floor.

My brothers know how important this night is to me, so it better not be either one of them calling him. He isn't sayin' anything to whoever is on the other end, but I can hear them barkin' even over the music.

"Alright, alright. I'm on my way," Rayvon said, catching my attention.

"Nikia, we gotta go," Rayvon said, grabbin' my hand and picking up his speed. I snatched my hand away from him and made my way back over to Black.

Black was sittin' with her cousins, Honesty and Heaven.

"Come on, Black. If you goin' with us, we're leaving," Rayvon spat as he stormed away.

"What the fuck is going on?" Black asked as she jumped up because she didn't want to be here anyway.

"I don't fucking know and I don't fucking care," I spat as we headed towards the door.

"Bitch, chill it's almost over anyways, you not missin' shit," Black said as we made it to the entrance where Rayvon is at impatiently waiting.

"We should have just come by ourselves," I said, and that pissed Rayvon off.

"Shnikia, don't fucking start," Rayvon insisted as he held open the door for me.

As we made our way to the limo, a black Nissan pulled up to the curb. No one has gotten out and they're just sitting there. Rayvon had called the limo driver, and he said he was coming and was only around the corner.

"Who the fuck is this in this car? Shnikia, get the fuck on!"

Rayvon yelled, and as soon as those words left his mouth, he pulled out his tool, and bullets started flying in his direction.

I hit the ground and started crawling back to the event center. I don't know who is screaming louder me or Black. I felt like the shooting was never going to stop, but when I heard a car skirting out the parking lot, I finally got the courage to lift my head. As I looked up, people started running out of the prom, screaming and hollering. I saw Rayvon laid out in the parking lot and blood is leaking from the holes that the bullets left. I jumped to my feet and ran as fast as I could over to him, dropped to my knees, cradling his head and as he stared off into space.

"Ray! Ray! Baby, please wake up! Baby, please wake up! I need you! Baby, please noooo!" I cried out, waiting for Ray to respond, but he wasn't.

My tears won't stop flowing, and even with Black holding me and telling me that everything is going to be okay, I know that it won't be.

"Nikia. Nikia!" Black called out as I shook Rayvon every so often in between holding his head, beggin' God to let him make it.

I know the life that he lives, but I never thought that I would end up here. I heard sirens, and as Black went off on these muthafuckas beggin' me to get up, I still didn't budge. I'm not leaving Rayvon. He never left me. Rayvon didn't even want to come to prom, but he knew how much it meant to me. This is all my fault; we shouldn't have come here. I'll never forgive myself.

2

SEVINO DAMAR THOMPSON

"Sevino, what about how the fuck I feel?" Lay Lay said as I put my shirt over my head.

"Blood, you knew what it was, and I don't have time to keep explaining to you what the fuck this is," I spat as I headed towards the door, and she jumped up running in front of me.

"Move," I spat.

"So, you just gon' leave?"

"Blood, move. I'm not fuckin' staying here and you already know that shit. Don't play dumb. Is you fuckin' stupid? On Bloods, move!"

"I'm dumb and stupid? Yeah, I'm dumb for ever fuckin' with you! Where are you going? It's not like you goin' to make no money. You a broke ass nigga, I don't even know why I fuck with you! I'm goin' to call that nigga Bloccc! He been tryin' to get with me, and I'm gon' let him take me out because yo' broke ass can't!"

"Bitch, for real? That nigga was yo' bro the otha day," I spat.

I pushed Lay out of my way and made my way out her momma's house. I walked down the walkway responding to my cousin Trumaine's text. Before I could hit send, he started call-ing, and I answered.

"Please don't leave, Vino. I'm sorry. Please don't go, why are you acting like this? I'm sorry. Please come back in."

"Bitch, get the fuck away from me," I spat as I turned around to face her.

"Sev—"

"Don't say my muthafuckin' name; go call that nigga Bloccc, hoe!" I spat.

"Nigga, where you at?" Trumaine asked.

"No, I don't want to call him. I didn't mean it and you know that."

"You flip floppin' ass bitch!" I spat as Trumaine told me he was around the corner.

Lay was beggin' me to come back in, but I'm not tryin' to hear that shit. Whatever the fuck you want to call what we had, it's over. After about two minutes of me tryin' not to catch a domestic, Trumaine pulled up to the entrance of the South Lincoln Projects.

I knew that fuckin' with Lay I was taking a chance. She's from the other side, but she lives over here on the West. Fuckin' was all that she ever got from me. I don't sleep at places that I don't pay bills at, that's not my thang, and she knows that. What the fuck I look like laid up in her momma's house? I fucked the bitch here because I need to re-up, so getting a room was out the question.

"I told you not to fuck with that bitch. You know where she's from," Trumaine said as I pushed Lay off me as she clung onto my arm.

I went to shut the car door and this dumb bitch put her arm in the way.

"Move that shit, Blood," I spat.

"No!" Lay yelled, still not moving.

As soon as she lifted it to where her hand was just in the

way, I slammed the door on that shit as hard as I could, twice, and jumped out the car, pushing her ass to the ground.

"Try holdin' that nigga dick with a broken hand, bitch," I spat and jumped back in the car.

"I told you about that bitch, and I told you not to fuck with her, nigga. Now look, you done had to break the bitch's hand."

"Nigga, shut the fuck up and take me to the house, so you can get back to stalking Ericka," I spat.

"Nigga, fuck you. I ain't stalking her," Trumaine insisted as he busted a left, heading towards the house.

"I'm not stalking her. That bitch wants me and you already know how the fuck we rockin'," Trumaine said, trying to convince himself because I know better.

This nigga been stuck on that bitch for as long as I can remember. The bitch grandma lived next door to us when we were fuckin' kids. The nigga never fucked the bitch. If he ever even seen the pussy, I'd be surprised, but just like Lay hoe ass, that bitch started flip floppin' and took her ass to the other side. This nigga was just pathetic and was still waiting even with a whole bitch and two kids. Sometimes I wonder how the fuck we were raised in the same fuckin' house.

"Nigga, I ain't stalking that bi..." Trumaine said as he pulled into the driveway at the house.

"Nigga, say it... She's a bitch. But nigga, she's not yo' bitch," I spat, getting out the car, shaking my head.

Me and this nigga done fought so many times over him being a fuckin' fien over that bitch. The way he just slammed the door to the Box Chevy that we went in on, I know he is feeling a fucking way. But I don't give a fuck. Why this nigga is stalking that bitch and her nigga, Enforcer? He needs to be more focused on gettin' some fuckin' money.

"Nigga, this is my fuckin' house!" Trumaine spat, making me laugh.

"Nigga, I pay the rent here. While you sending secret

admirer gifts to a bitch that won't speak to you in public, you fuckin' weirdo. What the fuck is wrong with you, nigga?"

"So, nigga, what's up? Trumaine said as he looked me up and down.

"Shit. nigga, what's up?" I spat.

"What the hell is wrong with y'all?" My auntie asked as she came from the back because I'm sure we woke her up.

"This nigga actin' like a bitch," I said as I sat down in the recliner.

"I'm actin' like a what?" Trumaine said, walking up on me.

I'm a little nigga compared to this nigga. I'm 'bout 5'7 and this nigga hoverin' over me, but he already knows I how I get down. If he wants to get it poppin' then we can. As this weirdo stood in front of me huffin' and puffin, I went to stand up, and the nigga rushed me back onto the chair, causing it to flip over.

"Nigga, you's a bitch!" I spat as we exchanged blows.

"What the hell is y'all doin'? No! Stop!" My auntie, Dawn, yelled as I took off on this hoe ass nigga.

"Stop! You know that Sevino is sick!" My auntie yelled as we went at it.

This nigga thinks because he is older than me that he knows what's best and how the fuck we should be moving, but taking this nigga's lead, I end up following Ericka and Enforcer around the fuckin' town.

This nigga is giving me body shots and I'm eating that shit. We fight all the time; this ain't nothin new, but lately, we fight when I tell him how the fuck he's living. He doesn't like when people call him out on his shit.

"Stooop! Right now or get the fuck out!" Auntie yelled, and Trumaine stopped swingin'.

He got up and bent down to offer me a hand, as I mugged his ass. I got up and Aunt Dawn stood in the middle of the living room floor with us, shaking her head with tears running down her face. I hate seeing my auntie like this. I turned my head so I couldn't see her face. She raised me since I was born. Her sister dropped me off over here when I was three days old and we ain't heard from her since.

"Don't even think about sitting down, pick up this shit that y'all done knocked over and talk this shit out," Aunt Dawn demanded, flopping down on the couch.

"Nigga, we blood," Trumaine said, breaking the silence.

"Yea, that's why you remind me that this is yo' house every chance you get, muthafucka!" I spat.

"Oh, you've said that before? Say it again. I wish the fuck you would. I dare you too," Auntie suggested.

I finished picking up the shit that we knocked over and made my way to the kitchen. I ain't mad because Trumaine wants to be a stalker. I'm mad because the shit that bitch Lay said was true. I'm on my dick and shit has just been fucked up. The little shit that I'm touching isn't enough to get me anywhere. A nigga runnin' in circles with Trumaine and my nigga Mailman by my side, but this nigga ain't making shit no better.

"I know that you gon' think that I'm crazy, but I know a way that we can get on. And be set," Trumaine said as he sat down at the kitchen table, and I looked up at him, all ears.

"I been scoping shit on the east side and we can get them niggas. I'm tellin' you we can make this shit shake."

"You go and rob Enforcer and Ericka on yo' own blood," I said as I left this muthafucka at the table.

3

SHNIKIA

"Nikia, you need to go. You won't forgive yourself if you don't. I know that this ain't easy, baby. I know exactly how you feel. I been there before, but baby, you need to go. Me and your brother will be there with you. And Black is goin' to be there for you too," my momma said as her and Black sat at the end of my bed.

"Why the fuck is you still in the bed? Get the fuck up and get dressed!" Bloccc barked as he barged in my room.

"She's getting' up," my momma said.

"You knew what the fuck it was. That nigga wasn't out here selling candy. Get the fuck up! Now!" Bloccc barked, now standing next to my bed, and the rage in his eyes and tone made my momma jump from the bed.

"Come on, baby. Get up," my momma said, pulling my arm.

"Get the fuck up now, Shnikia! I'm not fuckin' playin'! Wipe them fuckin' tears now!" Bloccc barked.

I got up, and once Bloccc seen me gathering up my stuff to get in the shower, he left the room. Bloccc is an asshole and has always been. He doesn't give a fuck about nothin'. I ain't scared of his big ass, but today I don't feel like arguing and fighting. My momma talks shit to everybody except Bloccc because of all that he does for her. Because he does so much for us, he feels like he's in control and makes all the rules, but he doesn't fuckin' run me. He does whatever the fuck he wants to in this house and my momma never says shit. Just like him just poppin' up over here whenever the fuck he pleases like today.

"What's wrong with Bloccc?" Black asked as she came walking in the room.

"Fuck Bloccc!" I screamed, so his big ass could hear me.

"What is going on?" Black asked as she plopped down on my bed and my momma left out.

I didn't answer because her ass knows how my stupid ass brother is. I made my way out my bedroom, so I can get this over with.

"Shnikia, don't muthafuckin' play with me I'll knock yo' head off yo' muthafuckin' shoulders. Keep fuckin' playin' with me, bitch and yo' ass will be laid next to that nigga where yo' stupid ass wants to be," Bloccc spat, stopping me from leaving out my room.

"Get the fuck out of my way!" I screamed as Black tried grabbing me back.

I hate this nigga. Big bad Bloccc, but them niggas that killed my daddy still breathing. He thinks that everybody is supposed to be scared of him. As he hovers over me, I can damn near see the steam coming out this nigga's ears.

Bloccc stands at 6'4 and weighs three hundred and some-thin' pounds. He has light skin like my momma's. I know that he'll fight me like a nigga in the streets and I'm just waiting for him to swing or maybe choke me out this time. I used to be terrified of this nigga, but now he knows that if I had balls, they hang just as low as his. Ain't no hoe in our blood and the way I'm feeling, I'll use the tool in my closet to take his big ass out.

Bloccc claims that he's hard on me because if he's not then I'll be a hoe and out here getting ran over by niggas and he's preparing for the real world. That's bullshit, he's the way he is because of how our father was with him and my momma. He used to beat Bloccc's ass and my mommas whenever he felt like it. Bloccc started acting out in school and fighting everybody he could when he was a kid. This nigga got unresolved daddy issues. He needs to take his ass to therapy and work that shit out.

I can tell looking up at his rosy cheeks, that he's been drinking. He knows that his bullshit took the only nigga that ever loved me correctly away from me. He'll never admit to me that Rayvon was killed because of his bullshit startin' shit with all these Westside Bloods for no reason, but I know that's what it was. The niggas that killed Rayvon didn't make it around the corner before they were caught, but I don't give a fuck about them going to prison. That does nothin' for me. Bloccc was muggin me hard and I'm matchin' his shit today. I haven't cracked a fuckin' smile since the night that my baby got killed a week ago.

"Y'all stop," Black suggested.

"Black, get the fuck out of here before I beat yo' muthafuckin' ass!" Bloccc barked.

"Go, Black!" I said, not taking my eyes off of Bloccc and she made her way out, squeezing past Bloccc.

"Get in the fuckin' shower and get yo' self together!" Bloccc spat, and his spit touched my face and then walked away.

"Yeah, nigga. At my momma's on Gilpin! Get over here now!" Bloccc demanded as I closed the bathroom door behind me.

～

"Sit the fuck up!" Bloccc barked as Black rubbed my back.

I looked back at him crazy, but I sat up straight and held my head high. Which is something I haven't done in a week. Bloccc already made all my tears go away. I fuckin' hate his big ass. I wish he would have died instead.

"I want to ask that we all keep the family in your prayers. The mother, Janet, Rayvon's girlfriend, Shnikia... all need you right now to keep them lifted in pra—" the preacher said as he was cut off.

"Girlfriend! What the fuck about me and his son!" A bitch yelled from the back.

"What about his fucking daughter that is a few weeks old!" Another bitch in the back yelled.

"What the fuck?" Black said, jumping up.

"Please, if you can't keep your outbursts to yourself, we're going to have to ask you to leave," The preacher said, but it was too late.

Bloccc jumped up and made his way to the back of the church. He wasted no time snatching what looks like a newborn baby girl out of the second bitch's arms and threw her damn near across the room. Luckily somebody caught her. He smacked the little boy to the ground and grabbed both the bitches, who were sitting right by each other, by their hair and drug them up to the front of the church where we are sitting.

"Oh my God! Stop!" Someone yelled.

"This is a church!" Someone else threw in.

"That nigga crazy. Bloccc will kill all of us," a nigga behind me said.

I looked down at the bitches as my brother held them by their hair up damn near putting them in me and Janet's lap as they begged him to stop. Janet hocked spit at both of the bitches one by one. I just want to leave right now, but I know that I'm going to have to fight Bloccc. Janet knew too, and she even had the audacity to hug me telling me that Rayvon loved me. My momma leaned in from the back of me and told me everything was going to be alright, but I knew that was far from the truth. I sat back crossing my legs as the funeral director came over to help us up to the casket. I shook my head no, and he left me alone.

As Lil' Wayne's, "I Miss My Dawgs," started playing, I fought back tears, and I got the chills. I watched Janet cling to Rayvon's casket damn near jumpin' it. Bloccc walked up on me and pushed Rayvon's aunt that has scooted down the pew, next to me. When she tried to rub me and console me, I stopped that shit fast. I barely know her ass; I don't want her touchin' me. Black came and sat on the other side of Bloccc. I've been sick and numb since Rayvon was killed.

As Lil' Wayne talked about Turk, all Rayvon's niggas rapped along.

"Are you sure that you don't want to see him before we close the casket?" The funeral director asked.

I shook my head no and Bloccc grabbed my arm tight.

"No," I said and Bloccc let go of my arm.

"You never let a muthafucka see you sweat! When you talking to anybody, you fuckin' answer. Remember who the fuck you is!" Bloccc spat as I zoned out, staring ahead of me with my eyes on the flowers in front of me.

I should have gone with my first mind and not came to this bullshit. This is so embarrassing. When the fuck did Rayvon have time to not only be fucking one bitch but two and has two whole babies. Here I am sick and not wanting to get out of bed sometimes but the whole time this nigga was playing me. As a woman sang, I checked the time on my phone. I just want this shit to be over already.

"Can we go now?" I asked Bloccc after a few minutes passed.

He stood up, and I followed suit and led the way down the church aisle as people looked on in fear. They wouldn't dare fix their mouths to say anything. If this nigga doesn't give a fuck about a newborn baby, he really doesn't give a fuck about nobody else. My momma rushed to my side, and as soon as she tried to hold me, Bloccc pulled her back.

"Keep yo' muthafuckin' head up!" Bloccc spat as I looked down at the floor for less than a second.

4

SEVINO

"Baby, I'm so sorry that I got stuck at work," Auntie said, rushing to my bedside.

"You're good, Auntie. I'm alright," I said, sitting up in my hospital bed.

My body was so sore and this crisis was wearin' me down. I've been dealing with this sickle cell shit since I was a baby. The doctors told Auntie I wouldn't make it to my first birthday, but here at twenty-three, a nigga still making it. This ain't the worst that I've seen with this illness, so I ain't complaining. Auntie stopped working when I was a kid to take care of me and make sure that I was good. She's been working for a few years now. And even with that, she calls me throughout the day to check on me because she's a worrywart.

"How was work?" I asked.

"It was work," Auntie said as somebody knocked on the door.

Shelly, the nurse, came in to check my vitals while doing her rounds. Shit, I come here so much I know all the damn nurses, the words they use and all the doctors in this bitch. I texted Trumaine to make sure he was in the spot because even though I can't be there, I need him to be so we can stay afloat. Shelly did her job and made her way out the room.

"Has that girl been up here to see you?"

"Naw, we're done," I said as I ignored Lay's call and turned off my ringer because she's been doing too much.

"Good."

I was done with Lay when she tried to clown me and bought up that nigga Bloccc. It's been three weeks since that night, and every day and night, this bitch is blowing up my phone. Me and Auntie sat talking and watching TV for a few hours 'til she fell asleep. As she slept, all I did was say my nightly prayer, praying for a brick. It may sound fucked up, but I got no other options. I dropped out in eighth grade. School wasn't for me and even with auntie beggin' me every day to get my GED, that shit ain't for me. What the fuck am I going to do, work a minimum wage job and then what? Because doing that shit alone, I wouldn't even be able to pay rent.

"Nigga, I don't want no fuckin' Chubby's," I said as Trumaine pulled up to his favorite spot.

"Nigga, we ain't ate this shit in days," Trumaine said as we got out the car and made our way in.

Like always, this bitch is packed after the club, and this is exactly why I don't like coming here — a bunch of drunk muthafuckas. As we got in line, these drunk bitches were standing in front of us. Well, this Black ass one for sure is because the thick one is damn near holding her up. They are talking all loud and shit, like they ain't standing right next to each other.

"Bitch, yes, go," the black ass one said.

"Nigga, I hate this fuckin' place," I reminded Trumaine in case he forgot.

"Excuse you, muthafucka," I spat as the thick bitch in front of me stepped on my fuckin' Jays.

"My bad," the bitch said and flipped her hair in my face as she turned around.

"This bitch," I spat.

"Nigga, who the fuck is you calling a bitch?" She questioned.

"You... bitch."

"Nikia, chill and come on. They called our number," the black ass one said, pulling her thick ass friend to the counter.

"Nigga, damn, it's packed in here. You trippin'," Trumaine said.

"Make sure my shit got extra chili on it," I said and made my way out before I have to smack a bitch.

After 'bout ten minutes, Trumaine finally made his way out. My phone was dry as hell. It ain't rang in a minute, which was fuckin' with me because I need some fuckin' money but Trumaine drunk ass ain't worried.

"Where the fuck is we goin'?" I asked as this nigga passed the house.

"Nigga, you need to relax and take a break from this money shit. We gon' be good," Trumaine insisted.

I started eating my food because I'm hungry and Trumaine's trying to eat his tacos and drive. It sounds good, but this nigga ain't had a plan yet that I would go with. He's the older cousin, but I can't fuckin' tell; this nigga is slow as hell. He thinks with his dick and that's where he fucks up at every time. In about twenty minutes, we made it to Aurora. Every time we come over here, it's some bullshit.

He pulled up to these ghetto ass apartments off Iliff. I ain't got shit against the hood, but I only fuck with my hood. This nigga Trumaine don't give a fuck where he goes.

"Who are these bitches?" I asked as we got out the car.

"It's cool. I got you. You gon' like the one that's for you," Trumaine insisted, which means I'm gon' hate the bitch.

"Nigga," I said as the black bitch from Chubby's opened the door.

Trumaine acted like he didn't hear me and hugged this bitch like he had known her for years. Ain't this a bitch, so I know that loud bitch ain't too far away. I sat on the couch, and Trumaine made his way to the kitchen with the black ass bitch. Then I seen him pouring more Hennessy into the cup he been drankin' out of since I got with this nigga. I pulled out my blunt because I'm going to have to be high to deal with this shit.

Then the rude bitch with the thick thighs and the fat ass came from out the back.

"I know that y'all didn't meet on good terms, but this is my best friend Shnikia and Shnikia, this is Sevino," Black ass said as she came walking back into the living room.

Shnikia folded her arms across her chest and rolled her eyes. I couldn't help but laugh and that made her even madder. I don't give a fuck. I sat back and finished smoking my blunt. We sat and Trumaine and Black ass drank for about thirty minutes. Shnikia didn't take her eyes out her phone. I smoked, waiting for my phone to ring.

"Let's play spades," Black ass suggested, claiming Trumaine as her partner.

I def peeped game that she's a runner and niggas definitely are running through her. Clearly the bitch does hair because she got a half ass hair salon set up where a dining room table should be. Shnikia ain't said one word, but she got up to play. I checked the time because I ain't stayin' here much longer. This bitch better know what the fuck she's doing.

As I dealt the cards and looked over at Shnikia, she looked like she doesn't know what the fuck she is doing. This nigga was being all lovey dovey with a hoe to get some pussy. This nigga was a clown.

"How many books you got?" I asked Shnikia.

"Five," she replied.

"Maybe three," she backtracked.

We started playin' even though I knew how this shit was goin' to play out. I checked the time, and we been playing for 'bout a half an hour, and these muthafuckas done set us every damn time. I got up to leave and Trumaine knew the deal and handed me the keys. I made my way outside to the car and jumped in.

Tap, tap, tap.

I pulled out my tool, before looking up and it's Shnikia's ass.

"Damn, you gon' shoot me?" She asked.

"What do you want, girl?"

"I just wanted to say sorry for the way I acted at Chubby's. I been going through a lot I—"

"Only a sorry muthafucka would say sorry," I spat and pulled out my parking spot.

5

SHNIKIA

"I don't give a fuck who drops dead in that bitch. Have yo' friendly ass out here on time, Shnikia," Bloccc spat we pulled up to my job.

I didn't respond. I just got out the car. I came out crying about Ms. Hope passing away and now everybody in the building is going to be next, let Bloccc tell it. As I made my way through the entrance, I was damn near knocked down by this bitch Nay trying to get outside to talk to Bloccc.

"Stupid ass bitch," I spat and made my way inside.

I made my way down the hall and was stopped by Ms. Mary and her daughter. She was supposed to be leaving. I took off last week, using my vacation time after graduation. If it wasn't for Bloccc and Black, I would have stayed in my bed the whole damn week. Bloccc sent me and Black to Miami for three days.

"My momma would not leave until you got here," Heather said as I hugged Ms. Mary.

"Ms. Mary," I said.

"You know I don't like these bitches especially Nay. Is she still chasing after yo' brother?" Ms. Mary asked, and we all started laughing.

I checked my watch and it's almost time for me to clock in, but I walked Ms. Mary and Heather outside. Ms. Mary was talking shit like she always does. I'm gon' miss her; she's been here a few times. With this being a rehabilitation center, a lot of times we end up seeing a lot of these people more than once. I got Ms. Mary in Heather's car and made my way back in.

"You always got to be doing extra, making the rest of us look bad," Nay whined.

"Do yo' fuckin' job, and you don't have to worry about what the fuck I'm doing," I spat as I clocked in.

"You have Ms. Matthews today and she needs a one to one," my supervisor Monica said.

I made my way to her room. It's going to be an easy day because she doesn't want much help. When I walked in her room and seen Sevino's rude ass, I started to turn right the fuck back around.

"This is the girl I was telling you about; you need a girl like her, Vino," Mrs. Matthews said.

"Hi, Ms. Matthews. Do you need anything?" I asked.

"No, Thickums, I'm fine, but I want to introduce you to my nephew Sevino," she sang.

"We know each other," Sevino said.

"Okay, I'll be right outside if you need anything," I said and left back out.

I went to go and make sure all the supplies are stacked because Nay is on camera watching all the patients in their room and the entire unit. so she'll let me know whether her bitch ass wants to or not if Mrs. Matthews needs me. I didn't think that I would see Sevino again. He was rude as hell the last time I seen him, and Black said Trumaine was a weirdo, so she kicked him out shortly after I left. I wasn't bout to stay there and be a third wheel. Other than hanging with Black, work is all I've been doing. Last week Bloccc sent me and my momma to Mississippi. I don't know what the fuck was going on, but I know it was some bullshit, so I was more than welcome to get the fuck out of here for a few days.

It's not a day that goes by that I don't think about Rayvon as much as I try not to. I still can't seem to shake the hold that he has on me. We had been together since ninth grade, so I don't expect to get over him tomorrow, but to have a day without any breakdowns would be nice. I can't believe how shit went down at the funeral. I never seen that coming. I never seen the signs that he was with other bitches, let alone had kids with 'em. I went from hurt to mad, and every day it's back and forth whenever our memories invade my mind.

"How are you doing, Nikia?" Monica asked as I stocked the shelves.

"I'm fine," I lied.

"Okay, but if you need some more time off, just let me know," Monica said, pattin' me on my back, which I fuckin' hate.

I don't like muthafuckas touchin' me and I damn sure don't want nobody pattin' me like a damn dog. Monica is cool and all, but I ain't telling her my damn business. I still can't believe she would fuck with Bloccc. She so damn smart, she's dumb. Because only a dumb bitch would fuck with him.

"Ms. Matthews needs you," Nay said as I walked past the nurse's station.

I made my way to her room and she wasn't in there, but Sevino was, so he had to push the button.

"Do you need something?" I asked.

"Yea, I just wanted to say thank you for the shit you've done for my aunt. She fucks with you," Sevino attempted to praise me.

"I'm just doing my job," I said and made my way out the room.

My phone started vibrating in my pocket and slippin' into the supply closer so I could see it was Black.

Black: Bloccc just left my house pickin' up this picked up head bitch lookin' so damn good. And if he wasn't so crazy, I would be yo sister-in-law, bitch!

Me: Bitch, bye!

Black has always had a crush on Bloccc. She can fuck up her life if she wants to. That bitch knows everything there is to know about him. The bitches and his crazy ass antics, so she's on her own with that shit. I don't want no parts in it. I just need to make it through this shift so I can go home and get in my bed with my new book.

～

"Hey, I know my nephew seems like an asshole, but he has a good heart. I don't know if you got a man or not, but Thickums, maybe y'all should go out," Ms. Matthews said, but before I could respond, Sevino walked in the room.

I'd be lying if I said he wasn't fine because he is. He has smooth chocolate skin, and tatted arms. Even though he's a lil' nigga, he definitely makes a difference in his appearance. The two times that we've crossed paths he had a mean ass facial expression; I never seen the nigga crack a smile. And as I glanced over at him before making my way out the room, this nigga stays high. From them glossy ass eyes and the stench that follows him when he comes in a room, mixed with his cologne, he's high now. We are about the same height, so he can't be more than 5'8. *He's plain and not flashy. Not even wearing a watch or chain,* I thought while checkin' my watch that Bloccc bought me for graduation. It's time for me to go.

I went to the break room to get my purse so I can head outside, but I got some time because I'm sure one of Bloccc hoes will be in the parking lot in his big ass face. So, I took my time heading out and sat down to read an email from the school about my financial aid.

"Girl, Ms. Matthews fine ass nephew is looking for you," one of my coworkers, Kelly, said as she came in the break room.

I ignored her and went back to reading my emails. I'm not on the clock and I know that my replacement is here, I seen the bitch come in. So she better go and help Sevino with anything that he needs because I can't do nothin' for him. I stayed in the break room for about ten minutes then made my way out, and Sevino was standing outside the door.

"Can I help you?" I asked as he just stared at me.

"Naw, but shit, I was thinkin' maybe we can exchange numbers and we can get together some time, but not with yo' girl Black," Sevino suggested.

"Naw, I'm good," I said as Sevino looked me up and down. I turned to walk away but was stopped when Sevino snatched my phone out of my hand.

"Give me my phone. I need to go," I said as he pressed buttons and ignored me.

After he was done doing whatever he wanted to do, he handed it back to me. I snatched it and made my way to the car as Bloccc started calling me.

6

SEVINO

I watched Shnikia's ass bounce as she walked down the hallway and from the way she's walking, she knew that I was watching. And when she looked back at me, she rolled her eyes and picked up her speed. She's cute, got a baby face, some pretty brown eyes, and this long ass weave down her back. These long ass different colorful ass nails. Thick as hell and that ass, I'd never forget. I just want to bend her over.

I made my way back into auntie's room and waited for her to get out of therapy, so I can get back to the spot. Trumaine is there, but I need to watch him to make sure the money is right. After a few minutes passed, Auntie made it back in the room. She fell at work and ended up here. If I don't do nothin' else, I'm gon' make sure auntie never has to work again real soon on Bloods.

"Did you talk to her?" Auntie asked as this lady helped her onto her bed.

A few minutes past, and this bitch is still in the room doing any and everything tryin' to get my attention. I'm tryin' to be cool and not go off, but this bitch is tryin' me. Now Shanay is standing here staring in my face. I don't know this bitch and I only know her name from her name tag. I'm not interested, and I don't care how many times she knocks somethin' over, so she can bend over to pick it up. These bitches kill me. Just do yo' fuckin' job.

"She's good. Bye," I spat.

"Damar!" Auntie yelled.

"What? Why is she still in here? You're good," I said and Shanay made her way out.

"You so damn rude, but when are you going out with Thickums?" Auntie asked, so excited.

"Auntie, I don't know," I said.

"Well, she's the one. You need somebody that ain't scared to call you out on yo' shit. I know why you go as hard as you do and I blame myself for that. If I was able to handle everything, then you wouldn't feel like you had to pick up my slack. And baby, I'm sorry for that, but when yo' momma left you with me, I promised myself that I would raise you like my own and give you everything you needed and wanted. But when your dad was killed, we lost everything that he was doing to help me with you," Auntie said.

"It's not yo' fault and you know that. I don't blame you for none of this shit. It's just what it is," I said as my phone started vibrating.

"Yea," I said, answering Trumaine's call.

"Nigga, I just got hit!" Trumaine yelled and started coughing uncontrollably.

"I'm on my way," I said, jumping up.

"You sure this is the street?" I asked my nigga, Mailman.

"Yea, this is it," Mailman insisted.

I pulled up on Giplin, stopped at the stop sign and sat there. One of Bloccc's niggas hit us, so I'm gon' hit him where it hurts.

I looked over at Trumaine with his busted-up face and fucked-up arm.

"Hop in the driver seat," I said to Trumaine. I threw the car in park, jumped out and ran around to the passenger side, and he ran around to the driver seat.

"Slow, I don't want nobody left in that bitch," I spat, and Trumaine followed my instructions.

Pop! Pop! Pop!"

Rat-a-tat-tat!

Pop! Pop! Pop!

"Empty the fuckin' clip!" I screamed out as Mailman followed my instructions.

The house was pitch black, and with it being after midnight, I'm sure everybody in there is sleeping. If it's up to me, they gon' all wake up dead. All that could be heard was glass shattering, shit breaking, and bullets flying. Once I emptied my clip and Mailman did the same, Trumaine drove off into the night.

"Run me by the house. I got some shit put up we can get off, so we can re-up," I said, and Trumaine made his way to the house.

Auntie will be home in a few days and the rent is due next week. Whatever the fuck I got to do to hold shit down, it's going to be done. Them East side bitches gon' feel me. And I'm not lettin' up, this is just day one.

We rode in silence, and the only thing that could be heard was the Boosie knockin' through the speakers. I got a lot of shit on my mind already and this is the last thing that I needed. We pulled up at the house after about twenty minutes and I ran in the house to get my shit and back out just as fast.

"Did you think about the shit I said the other day?" Trumaine asked.

"Naw but tell me everything that you know about the bitch and her nigga," I suggested.

Right now, something gotta shake because this shit ain't working. As Trumaine laid out everything about Ericka from her schedule to where the bitch eats breakfast on Fridays, I knew that this nigga was crazier that I thought and needs to get some help. As soon as I can, I'm gon' send this nigga to a therapist or somethin'. But right now, I need to know everything so that I can set this shit up right so me and Mailman can handle it. Trumaine told me everything he knew about the bitch and her nigga, including some shit I wish he would have kept to himself.

We pulled up to the spot and made our way in as Trumaine passed me his phone, saying somebody wanted to talk to me. It was just the muthafucka that I needed to talk to.

7

SHNIKIA

"You can't fuckin' stay here. I don't know what part of that you don't get! It's not a fuckin' option!" Bloccc yelled, making my momma jump.

"I don't want to stay at yo' fuckin' house!" I screamed, rubbing my eyes.

"Then take yo' ass to the park!" Bloccc spat and disappeared to the back of the house.

"This is all his fuckin' fault. This is his shit, why niggas are shootin' up the fucking house!" I yelled while my momma tried to calm me down.

"It's my fault, hun? Who the fuck you think pays bills the rent and keep the lights on over here, hun?" Bloccc yelled as he ran into the room pushing me into the wall, making our childhood picture crash to the ground that were barely hanging on since it was bullet riddled.

"Nigga, and that means that I should be thanking you! I don't need shit from you; I promise you that!"

"Pack yo' shit and get to the fucking truck now, Shnikia!" Bloccc spat, punching a hole in the wall next to my head.

My momma ran into my room, so I know she's packing my

stuff. I made my way to the porch, with my damn pajamas on, scarf tied on my head and my phone and purse. I'm, so sick of this shit. It's always some bullshit and Bloccc is the reason. All his niggas are posted up in the front yard. Where the fuck was these niggas when somebody was spraying the house with bullets? Trigga was pacing back and forth up and down the street. If he wasn't up his bitch's ass, then he would have been here.

My momma ran out the house with her hands full of our stuff. I took my time walking over to Bloccc's truck. Bloccc snatched open the back door and went over to open my momma's door. By the time I made it to the truck, Bloccc jumped in, slamming his door, making the windows shake.

As we drove, all I could think about was the fact that I have to either get my own shit or live with Bloccc. He lives in Centennial, so we are nowhere near our house on the East side. I don't want to fuckin' stay at his house. I hate when he comes to our house every day, so to have to live with him is going to be hell.

I texted Black back to tell her we were going to Bloccc's, so she can pick me up from there tomorrow. My momma keeps looking back at me and Bloccc was muggin' me in the rearview mirror. I rolled my eyes and sat back because I know that this shit is about to get thick.

～

"WHAT THE FUCK HAPPENED LAST NIGHT?" Black asked as I got in her car.

"Bloccc said it was some West side niggas," I said, shrugging my shoulders and turning up the music because I don't feel like talking.

"Is your mom in there?" Black asked and I nodded my head.

I just want to go to the house, so I can grab some more of my stuff and go to Black's, so we can go out tonight. I need to do

somethin' to get my mind off of this shit. My momma is going to
ride with whatever Bloccc says, and I'm not staying with him
for long if I decide to stay at all. I got some money saved up, and
if I have to get my own place, then that's what I'm going to do.
Because Bloccc and all his damn rules and bullshit, I'll pass on
all that. My momma gon' do whatever Bloccc says, so I'm not
even going to talk to her about getting our own place because
she'll try to talk me out of it.

When we pulled up to the house, Trigga was sittin' on the
porch with his tool on his lap. I jumped out and made my way
in. Bloccc cussed him out half the night because he wasn't here
when shit went down. I don't know why the fuck he sittin' out
here now, what's done is done and the only thing they did was
fuck up the house and kill Bloccc's fuckin' dogs. Me and my
momma were lucky to make it out of there still breathing. I
looked around my room at all the bullet holes that came so
close to where I normally lay, but I just so happened to fall
asleep on the couch last night.

I grabbed up some of my work clothes and a couple pairs of
shoes. When I looked up, Trigga was standing in the doorway.

"What?" I asked because he ain't sayin' shit.

"You can just come with me to Tay's," Trigga offered.

"I'll pass," I said as I made my way out.

"I know you don't want to be at Bloccc's, Nikia, and you
don't want to be around Tay or her fuckin' sister and 'em, but
I'll let both them bitches know what it is. They won't even say
shit to you if that's how it needs to be."

I can't believe that he would even ask me that shit knowing
that Tay's sister Symone was the bitch that showed up at Ray's
funeral with the little girl. Why the fuck would I want to be
around Tay knowing how close her and her sister are? Trigga
wants to be Bloccc so bad, but I'm convinced he's kinda slow,
and Bloccc reminds him of that every chance he gets. Trigga is
the baby and should be in the tenth grade, but he gave up on

school along time ago and just wanted to run the streets with Bloccc.

"So, what you want to do tonight?" Black asked as I got in the car.

"I need to figure out what I'm going to do with my life," I admitted.

"Well, bitch, you ain't gon' figure it out tonight. I told you that you can come and stay with me until you find something and bitch, you already know how your brother is. He's not going to change, Nikia," Black said, rolling her eyes.

I need my space, and when I don't want to be bothered, I want to be able to be left the fuck alone. And staying with Black in her one-bedroom, I'm not going to have that option. So, when I get mad or sick of Black, I'll still have to look at her ass, not to mention the hoes who hair she does. She made her way to her house while my mind was running a mile a minute, weighing my options.

After about ten minutes, Black pulled up at the gas station down the street from her house.

"You want something out of here?" Black asked.

"Naw, I'm good," I said as I looked over out the window, and Sevino pulled up on the side of us.

"Damn, so you ain't gon' call me?" Sevino asked as he got out of his car.

The last time I seen him, he took my phone and called his phone, but with all that's been going on, the last thing that has been on my mind is a nigga. Especially his rude ass. I'm fuckin' homeless. Well, not real homeless but damn near as far as I'm concerned. I didn't respond to Sevino, so he snatched open my door.

"Blood, I know you can hear, so you ain't gon' answer my question?" Sevino asked, invading my space.

"I'm not calling you. For what?" I asked, wishing he would go in the store and get the fuck out my face.

"Come ride with me," Sevino suggested as Black came out the gas station.

"I'm good," I said., Then he reached over, unbuckled my seatbelt and grabbed my hand, snatching me up out the car.

"Nigga, are you crazy?" I asked, snatching away from him.

"A little," he said as a smirk spread across his face.

"Nigga, I'm not going nowhere with you. I don't even know you," I spat, leaning against Black's car.

"You should go. You need to relax and clear your head, just call me," Black suggested like she was trying to get rid of me.

What the fuck do I have to lose? At this point, if he gets on my nerves too bad, I'll call Black to come and get me. I know that she must have got a call or text and was itchin' to get to whoever it was requesting her attention. I don't want to go to Bloccc's tonight, so if Sevino can prolong that, I'll play this game with him. I snatched away from Sevino, and he opened the passenger side door of his car, and he went into the gas station.

My phone started vibrating and it's Black, like she's not right next to me in her car.

Black: Have fun and be nice to him, bitch!

I stuck up my middle finger at her and she pulled out her parking spot. I guess she's right. I do need to relax, but I don't know nothin' about this nigga. The last thing I need is a nigga and his fuckin' problems bringing more to me than I already have to deal with.

Shit, this nigga ain't that fine!

I watched him go off on all the workers in the damn gas station. I don't know what the fuck they did to him, but he's pissed. The girl that was behind the counter ran from behind the counter and to the back of the store. Clearly this wasn't a good idea. This nigga doesn't even know how to act a gas station.

"I thought I was gone have to come down the street to Black's to get you," Sevino said as he got in the car.

"What took you so long in there?" I asked.

"Long story."

"Nigga, I got some time."

I waited for him to tell me what happened, but he didn't say shit and his eyes are glued to the road.

"Where are we going? Because I got something to do tonight." I said, folding my arms across my chest.

"I bet," Sevino said, glancing over at me.

"I'm not 'bout to hang around yo' weird ass cousin," I said as Sevino jumped on I-225 N.

"Just sit back," Sevino requested, placing his free hand on my thigh.

I snatched away because I don't know what the fuck he thinks this is, but this ain't that. He laughed and kept driving. As we talked, I realized how different we are. I'm not into all that bangin' shit with my brothers, but I do know that if they knew I was with this Blood nigga, not only would they try to take my head off, he'd be stretched out right next to me. I would never tell no nigga who my brothers are. I haven't even thought about entertaining nobody since Rayvon was killed.

The only reason why I'm even with this nigga now is to try to get my mind off all the bullshit. I was woke up out of my sleep this morning with messages from one of Rayvon's baby mommas, Tay, asking me for money. Saying all types of shit. I started to tell Bloccc, but I just deleted her messages and didn't waste my time responding. I wish the fuck I would give that bitch or any other bitch anything that I had from Rayvon. The bitch was a well-kept secret, her and her baby, so as far as I'm concerned, her best bet is to stay one. If she knows what's best for her.

After about thirty minutes of us talking and Sevino being

real careful with what he reveals we pulled up to this Mexican Restaurant in Lakewood called *Jose O'Sheas*.

"You like Mexican food, don't you?" Sevino asked as he got out the car and came over to let me out.

"It's a little too late if I don't, ain't it?" I said, shutting the door.

"Well shit, don't eat," Sevino's disrespectful ass suggested.

We walked in, and the hostess led the way shortly after to our table. I've never been here, but Sevino seems pretty comfortable, so he must have been here before.

"Your waitress will be with you shortly," the hostess said and damn near ran away.

This nigga must have fucked her before.

I started looking over the menu. When I looked up as I flipped it over, Sevino was staring at me. I rolled my eyes and went back to looking at the menu. A few minutes passed and I think I know what I'm going to get.

"Where the fuck is the waitress?" Sevino spat.

"Umm, maybe helping these other people."

"One of the bitches better get over here to take our order," Sevino damn near yelled, causing the white people next to us, eyes to damn near buck out their heads.

"Would you shut up!" I suggested.

"I'm not!" Sevino yelled.

"I can't believe you are from the East side," Sevino said, catching me off guard.

"What the fuck is that supposed to mean?" I asked as the waitress walked up and took our order.

"You don't act like the bitches I know from over that way," Sevino said, shruggin' his shoulders once the waitress hurried away.

"You don't know me. You don't know shit about me."

"Stay with me tonight."

"What? Nigga, I don't even fuckin' know you. Fuck no I'm not staying with you tonight," I spat.

"Well, yo' ass ain't going home. So, unless you one of them bitches from the East that

calls the police, you ain't going nowhere," Sevino insisted as the waitress bought out our drinks.

My phone started vibrating. I checked my caller id, it's Bloccc.

Bloccc: Where you at?

Me: Out

Bloccc: You need to check in and let me know where you are at, Shnikia. If you leave Black's.

Me: I'm grown as fuck! If you want somebody to tell what to do, I suggest you have a baby!

I ignored Bloccc's message that came through and gave my attention back to Sevino, who hasn't taken his eyes off me.

"Why don't you drink or smoke?" Sevino asked, catching me off guard.

"My momma does enough of that for everybody," I admitted.

He nodded his head. The waitress brought chips and salsa over to us, and he started munchin' on em.

"Who was that texting you? Yo' nigga?" He asked with an attitude.

"If I had a nigga, I wouldn't be here with you," I spat.

"It sounds good," Sevino said, suggesting that he didn't believe me.

"So how many bitches and kids you got?" I asked, not wanting no surprises.

"I don't got no bitches and I don't got no damn kids," Sevino answered, showing his irritation.

The waitress bought out our food and then hauled ass away from our table. Why the fuck the people in here runnin' away from this nigga?

"How many of yo' bitches have you taken here?" I asked in between taking a bite of my chimichanga.

"Just one?"

"Umm, what's her name?"

"Shnikia."

"Nigga, I'm a whole lot of things, but yo' bitch ain't one of 'em!"

He ignored my response and started askin' too many damn questions for me. I answered his questions selectively and he answered mine with rude ass responses. When we finished eating, he paid the check, then we made our way out the restaurant. He opened my door, so I could get in the car.

"So, you can take me to Black's?" I said as he got in the car.

"I'm not," he spat.

8

SEVINO

"I should be a matchmaker. I need to charge you for my services," my auntie bragged as I walked in the house from taking Shnikia to work.

"Naw, auntie. This isn't that," I said.

"Don't try to downplay Thickums. She been at this house damn near every day for the past month. I know that this is the first girl you ever brought over here. And, nigga, I'm not dumb; I know that she been sleeping here."

"Alright, auntie," I said as I made my way through the house.

She's exaggerating; it ain't been that often. She has been at the house here and there, but not like Auntie tryin' to make it seem. She doesn't ask no bunch of questions getting on my damn nerves. Shnikia is cool, and I ain't never heard of her, so I know she ain't out here like that. I don't like that she from the East, but she made it clear she ain't got no ties to the streets, so I ain't trippin'. And tonight, when I pick her ass up from work, I'm gettin' some pussy.

"Nigga, are you done playing house today so we can get back to business?" Mailman asked as I walked into the kitchen.

"Shut the fuck up," I spat as I sat down at the table and ran the play through my head a dozen times.

"Nigga, we been going through this shit for how long now? We're ready, and if we not, we don't have any other options, we have to make some shit work," Mailman insisted.

I felt a way about keeping this shit from my cousin, but at the rate he be going, who knows what the fuck could happen if I let him bring feelings in. It's just the way shit had to be for now.

"Tonight at midnight." I reminded Mailman, just in case he forgot.

"Nigga, I'll be ready. You just be ready."

"Nigga, I stay ready."

"Shit, I don't know, nigga. If you out there taking bitches on dates and shit."

"I bought the bitch some Burger King."

"What, nigga? Today? Because y'all damn sure been more places than Burger King. Nigga, I've known you damn near my whole life, and you ain't never bought me shit."

"Alright, Blood. Come on, I'll buy you something to eat."

Shnikia was cool and we been kickin' it. I took her to the house because my money is tight and Auntie fucks with her, so I know she wouldn't care. Right now, my only focus is this lick that me and Mailman have on the floor for tonight. Everything else can wait.

∼

"YOU SURE THIS IS THE HOUSE?" I asked, turnin' off my ringer because Shnikia was calling.

"This is it. The house that Trumaine said they come in and out of all day, and that's Envii's truck," Mailman said, referring to Ericka by the name that nigga Enforcer gave her.

I slid my mask over my face and Mailman, caught my attention, "What the fuck? Nigga, is that Trumaine?" Mailman asked, hitting the dashboard as I watched Trumaine kickin' in the front door to one of Ericka's spots that I planned for us to hit.

"Did you tell that nigga what the fuck we were doing?" I spat.

"Hell naw, I ain't say nothin' to that nigga. You know how that nigga moves when it comes to that bitch. Shit, I was with you with keepin' that nigga on the outs."

"Fuck!" I spat, hitting the steering wheel.

As Trumaine ran out the house with two bags and I clutched my tool, I just don't believe this shit is so easy. There is no way that Ericka is in that house. Just as Trumaine jumped in the car with his baby momma and skirted off, I seen this nigga Murk come out the house. Murk is Ericka's cousin. That is the only reason why this shit went so smooth. Murk has always been soft, he'll beat a bitch from Sunday to Sunday, but when it comes to a nigga, that nigga bitches up every time. I removed my mask, Mailman did the same, and I pulled away from the curb.

"You gotta get over there fast, nigga because the way he moves when it comes to bitches, he been done fucked it all up," Mailman said as I tried to catch up with Trumaine and that bitch.

I'm addicted to money, and that shit wakes me up everyday, even dealing with this sickle cell shit, but Trumaine is motivated by pussy. He lets pussy control all of his moves. I can hear that bitch giving out instructions, and we haven't even made it to the house yet. Mailman talked his shit and after about ten minutes, we made it to Wanii's house. My phone started ringing, and it's my auntie, so I answered.

"Damar, where the hell are you at? I know you seen Thickums calling you!" Auntie yelled in my ear, and I know she mad because she is calling me Damar.

"I'm handlin' something. I told Shnikia I'd be back in a second when I dropped her off."

"She's fuckin' worried about ya black ass! Somebody just got killed in the Lincoln Projects."

"Tell her I ain't over there. I'll be there in a minute," I said and hung up on my auntie as she went off.

"Damn, what the fuck you do to her, she already blowin' up yo' shit and got auntie calling and shit," Mailman clowned as we got out the car.

"Bitch, you asked me could I sit here why you went and got my money out the ATM, what fucking ATM did you go to?" Black ass yelled as I walked up the walkway.

I shook my head as Black kept going off on Wanii's dumb ass. Looking at her, I see that Black ass must have done her hair, and she left the kids with her while she drove Trumaine to the lick. I know she doesn't even know Black ass like that because Trumaine fucked her ass the night we were at her house. Black ass ain't the type to blow up the spot from what I've seen of her since I been kickin' it with Shnikia. She's all about her bread.

When I walked into the kitchen, Trumaine was laying the money and dope that he just got out on the table. He didn't even realize that me and Mailman were in the kitchen.

"What the fu—" Trumaine said as he looked up at us, with his tool in his hand.

"You weren't gon' tell us what the fuck you was doing?" I asked as I leaned against the sink and Mailman sat down across from him at the kitchen table.

"You wasn't tryin' to hear what the fuck I been telling you. I told you that I could set this shit up and you didn't list—"

"Before you get to planning shit with these niggas. I need what the fuck you promised me?" Wanii screeched as she came in the kitchen.

"I gave you money to get yo' hair done," Trumaine replied.

"Nigga, it sounds good. Now give me my money!" Wanni yelled.

"Bitch, get the fuck out the kitchen, and you'll get whatever the fuck you gon' get in a minute," I spat.

"This is my fuckin' house, Sevino! You don't tell me what the fu—"

"Bitch, you don't pay real fuckin' rent here. I said get the fuck out the kitchen, and I don't repeat myself to nobody but old people and kids, bitch!" I spat as I rushed over to her.

She stared at me, wishing, hoping and praying that her nigga stood tall for her, but we both knew that wasn't going to happen. Blood is thicker than water when it comes to me and Trumaine any day. She huffed and puffed and made her way out the kitchen.

"None of yo' bitches respect you," I spat as I sat down at the table.

"Nigga, fuck you. I made this shit happen without yo' fuckin' help. Here's the money that I lost when I got hit. Since you made sure Momma was good, but nigga, this is mine," Trumaine spat.

"Nigga, fuck you and that money. And when that bitch kicks you out because she will and nigga, you know it, when you fuck over this shit because you're going to. Nigga, don't come lookin' for me then," I spat and made my way out.

"Ayye, Blood, wait a second," Mailman called out from behind me.

I just kept walking and was tempted to punch Wanii in her shit on my way out, but the only thing that saved her was Lil' Trumaine sitting in her lap. I made my way out with Mailman following close behind. I'm not gon' stop Mailman from gettin' in with him on that shit, but I'm not having no parts in that shit I'll figure something else out. Like I've been doing.

"Nigga, fuck that bitch, and you know that's her puttin' that shit in his head," Mailman said as we stepped out on the porch.

"I'm not gon' stop you from eating off that shit, but I'm good," I said, wanting no parts.

"Hun, take this," Mailman said, handing me an ounce of dope he had left from our shit.

I took it, we shook up, and I left. That's just the type of nigga that Mailman is. He's solid and I can always count on him to come through. He one of the niggas that if you're broke and he got it, he'll make sure that you're good and you gon' eat if he eats. My phone lit up and I looked down at it.

SHNIKIA: THE LEAST YO' MUTHAFUCKIN' ASS COULD DO IS ANSWER MY FUCKING CALLS! I JUST WANTED TO KNOW THAT YOU WERE OKAY! IF YOU WERE GOING TO BE GONE THIS FUCKIN' LONG, I COULD HAVE WENT HOME! STUPID MUTHAFUCKA!

9

SHNIKIA

"Take me home!" I screamed, jumping up off the bed as Sevino came into his room.

"Lower yo' fuckin' voice," Sevino said, too damn calm for me.

"I'm not doing shit! Take me home!" I screamed. He rushed over to me, now standing so close that I could smell the Kush and cologne mixture that he always has that makes my pussy wet every time I'm in his presence.

"Shut the fuck up," Sevino spat, wrapping his arms around me.

"Get o—" I attempted to say as Sevino pressed his lips against mine, pushing me back and making us fall on the bed.

Every time I tried to break our kiss, Sevino would stop me with his tongue. This isn't the first time that we've kissed, and a part of me feels bad because I shouldn't be here. That's why I've stopped it from going any further previous times. It has barely even been a month since I buried the only man that I have ever loved, and I thought that my heart was broken when the doctor told me that Rayvon didn't make it, but when them bitches popped up at the funeral, it was shattered.

"I can't do this," I said as Sevino started sucking on my neck.

"What you talking 'bout? Shut up Nikia," Sevino said as he stuck his tongue in my ear, causing me to clench my thighs tighter as he sent chills up my spine.

"Damar!" I cried out in pleasure.

"You been spending too much time with my auntie," Sevino said, looking down at me.

Sevino ripped my tank top off me in one swift motion and yanked off my pants. As he kissed every part of my body, my mind started to race, wondering if I was making a mistake. I shouldn't be here. I need to just go to Black's. With each kiss, Sevino was tearing down the walls that I tried to put up to protect my heart from him. Even though he's rude as hell and is in the streets so much, he's been a real stress reliever whenever I'm around him. I've never met a nigga who wasn't scared to talk shit back to me.

Sevino twirled his tongue all over my stomach. As he kissed my pussy through my panties, I grabbed the back of his head. He ripped my panties off me and flicked his tongue over my clit, making me lose my breath. Every time I think he's going to stop, he keeps goin' as my legs started shakin'. I threw my head back onto the bed and became weaker than I already was as he started hummin' on my pussy.

I locked my legs around his neck as he just kept goin' makin' me cum. He kissed his way up my body with his dick poking me. I managed to look down at it while trying to recover. When this nigga took off his clothes, I do not know because I damn sure missed that. Sevino kissed me as he slid into me, catchin' me off guard because I wasn't prepared for his ten inches. I don't think that no amount of time would have prepared me for it.

As he slow stroked me while staring in my eyes, I closed my eyes, and that just made him pick up his speed.

"Fuck," I cried out as he started goin' deeper with my legs on his shoulders.

"Damn, Nikia," Vino moaned out as he pushed one of my legs towards me, while letting the other down to my side and started givin' my pussy long and hard strokes.

We fucked forever, and my damn legs were useless after we finally finished. Sevino fell right to sleep while holding me tight. I couldn't seem to fall asleep as the reality of what I just did sank in. I started crying thinkin' 'bout Rayvon. I was scared that Sevino would wake up, so I got up and threw on one of his T-shirts and made my way to the bathroom.

"So, you just moved over here? You don't even got a fuckin' room," Bloccc barked as I came into the living room at Black's.

I haven't even been here except today, and the only reason why I'm here now is because I feel guilty for fucking Sevino. He's cool, but I shouldn't have done that to Rayvon. It was wrong, and I couldn't even look at Sevino anymore. I left while he was sleep and had Black come pick me up.

"Umm, muthafucka, I know yo' ass heard me!" Bloccc yelled.

"What difference does it make? I'm grown. I'm eighteen, Bloccc. You can't tell me where the fuck I can and can't go," I spat as I sat at the barstool at the island that separates the living room and the kitchen.

"Look, I know that you don't want to be at my house, and I don't want yo' crybaby ass at my house either, but right now, I need to make sure that you're good. And I need to know where the fuck you're at. At all fuckin' times!" Bloccc ordered.

"Did you find them niggas that shot up my momma's house?" I asked as I turned around on the stool to face him.

Bloccc rushed me like we were on a fuckin' football field and wrapped his arm around my neck, squeezing as tight as he could, taking my breath away.

"Bloccc, stop!" Let her go!" Black screamed, rushing over to us and pullin' Bloccc's shirt but not even fuckin' with his grip on my neck.

Knock, knock, knock.

"Bloccc, stop! My client is here! Bloccc, let her go!" Black yelled, and Bloccc flung me to the ground so hard that I hit my head hard causing me to become dizzy and blurring my vision.

When Black dropped down to make sure that I was good, Bloccc stormed out the house opening the door so hard it smacked into the wall and came off the hinges.

"What the fuck did my door do to you, muthafucka?" Black screamed as she helped me off the ground.

Her client walked in looking at me crazy as hell, so I made my way back to Black's room, shutting the door behind me. My phone was ringing on the nightstand. I picked it up.

Sevino: Where the fuck you at?

Me: I'm at Black's.

Sevino: Damn, so you just leave without saying shit?

I put my phone down because I'm not gon' come to him as some broken, confused bitch. He knows nothin' 'bout Rayvon. I would never discuss him with Sevino. I haven't told him nothing about my brothers or the other side. It didn't take long for me to realize that he was a Blood through and through. I don't care about none of that shit, that's my brothers on that Crip shit. I don't want no parts in that.

"Bitch, wake up, yo phone keeps going off!" Black yelled, waking me up.

"It's just Sevino," I said as I looked at my phone and put it right back down.

"You fucked him?" Black said, and I put the pillow over my head.

"You fucking whore!" Black screamed and then busted out laughing.

I took the pillow off of my head and fanned the smoke cloud that I was in, in this damn room. Thanks to Black. I know that I shouldn't feel bad, but I do. No matter how much I try to hate Rayvon for the bullshit that he did to me, I still love him and probably always will. Sevino is cool, and even with his pockets not being that big, he gives me his time.

Sevino has been taking me to and from work. He brings me lunch and texts me throughout the day. He doesn't want me sitting in the spot with him and I love that shit because I don't want to be nowhere near that part of him.

"Bitch, you fucked him, so what! Shit you gotta live yo' fuckin' life or you should have jumped in that casket with his ass like Bloccc told you to," Black said in between laughing.

"I love Rayvon, Black."

"Bitch, I love Mike, Big Maniac, and Bloccc. Bitch, you know I love Bloc—"

"Bitch, I'm being serious right now," I whined.

"Bitch, what? I do love Bloccc, for real. But this ain't about me and me being yo' sister-in-law right now. You gotta keep living yo' life. Shit, you never know what the fuck is going to happen. What the fuck you gon' do, just work yo' ass to death. And throw yo' self into school. Shit, that ain't gon' work, and I'm not gon' let you. So, you can take a break from Sevino and come out with me and Big Maniac and Lil' Maniac tonight?"

"Bitch, I'm not," I spat and rolled over as my phone lit up on the nightstand.

Boom!

"What the fuck is that?" Black asked as we both jumped up, staring at her bedroom door as it flew open.

"You been fucking with some fucking Blood niggas, bitch!" Bloccc barked as he snatched me up by my neck and threw me onto Black's bed, holding me by my throat tighter than he did earlier.

10

SEVINO

"You good?" Mailman asked as I lit my black.

I nodded my head and slipped my phone back in my pocket. It's been a month since I seen or heard from Shnikia. She called me crying about her brother, so I went to Black's and got her. But when she got with me, she didn't want to talk about whatever happened. I respected that and left the shit alone. We went, got something to eat, and she stayed the night. The next day I took her to work and haven't heard from her since. I went to pick her up, like I always do, and she wasn't there. I called her, and she didn't answer. I texted and still not shit.

"Sevino!" Auntie yelled from inside the house.

"Yea, what's wrong?" I asked as I walked in the house, looking at her with these papers in her lap and eyes full of tears.

"Sit down. baby," Auntie suggested, so I sat down as Trumaine walked through the door and bullets started zooming past our heads.

Rat-a-tat-tat.

Pop! Pop! Pop!

Auntie hit the ground as I ran outside, walking over to

Trumaine as he bled out in the doorway. Mailman was front in center bustin' back at them niggas as I joined in. They hit Mailman in his shoulder and he still kept letting his Glock bang. They skirted off down the street as I ran back in the house and seen my Auntie cradling Trumaine like he was a newborn.

~

"NIGGA, I'm good. What's going on with Trumaine?" Mailman asked as his momma got up to leave the room.

"He's gon' be good," I said, not able to believe it myself.

"Damn, they hit that nigga five times, and he still here. That nigga's Teflon!" Mailman joked.

"Teflon for sure. I'm gon' let you kick it with yo' mom and sister and shit, and I'll get back with you before I leave," I said standing up to go and check on my auntie.

We been at this fuckin' hospital since yesterday. Shnikia remembered my number and been blowing up my shit since we got up here but I don't got shit to say to her. Wherever the fuck she been is where the fuck her ass can stay. I made my way down the hall to Trumaine's room and Shnikia was sitting on the other side of his bed.

"Why the fuck is you here?" I spat as I walked in the room.

"I'm he—"

"I don't give a fuck why you are here. Bye, muthafucka! Go on back to where the fuck yo' ass been at!" I spat as I made my way over to her grabbing her by her arm.

"Damar, stop! Let her fucking go!" Auntie screamed.

"Don't put yo' fuckin' hands on me!" Shnikia screamed, snatching away.

"Get the fuck out," I spat. Shnikia pushed past me and made her way out with my auntie right behind her.

"Why the fuck is you doing that girl like that? She really

fucks with you, nigga. Why the fuck else would she be here?" Trumaine said, turning down the TV.

"Nigga, I don't need no advice on how to handle bitches from you, Teflon," I said, referring to him as the name that Mailman gave him.

"Nigga, for real. No bullshit."

"Nigga, you know so much about bitches, where the fuck is yours?" I asked, looking around for Wanii, who is nowhere to be found.

I sat and talked to Trumaine about who the fuck it could have been that shot him and Mailman. After about an hour, Auntie still ain't been back in here. Where the fuck is she at? Her or Shnikia don't drive, so I know she gotta be in this hospital somewhere.

"Where the fuck my momma go?" Teflon asked, and I got up to go find her.

I made my way out to the lobby and pepped them across the room. As I walked over to them, I could hear them talking, and I want to know why auntie fucks with her ass so hard because clearly, she ain't the bitch we thought she was.

"Baby, I know it's not going to be easy, and now isn't the time, but you need to tell him," Auntie said.

"Tell me what?" I asked as I walked up on them and the sound of my voice made Shnikia jump.

"Go outside and talk," Auntie suggested.

Looking around the lobby, this bitch was packed, so I damn sure ain't talking about shit in here. I turned to leave out and Shnikia came after me. I can hear her crying, but I don't give a fuck about none of that shit. I got my own shit going on, so she can save that shit for whatever nigga she been with.

Once we made it outside and on the sidewalk in front of the hospital, I turned around to face Shnikia.

"What the fuck you need to tell me?" I asked.

"When I told you the last night that I was with you that me

and my brother had gotten into it, it was about me being with you. It was some shit that I didn't tell you. I'm not in that shit with my brothers, and I can't stop them from doing what they do. And—"

"And what, Shnikia? Quit playing with me. What the fuck is you talking 'bout? Spit it out!"

"Bloccc is my brother and —" Shnikia attempted to say but I cut her off.

"Stay the fuck away from me. Don't call me, don't text me and don't come nowhere near me," I spat and walked away.

I can't believe this shit. Out of all the bitches in the world, I get caught up with Bloccc's sister.

"Damar!" Shnikia cried out.

11

SHNIKIA

I knew that coming up here was going to be a risk and that is exactly why I have been staying away from Sevino. The night when Bloccc busted into Black's and dragged me into the parking lot, he beat the fuck out of me. When Black tried to help me, he ordered one of his niggas to hold her. Bloccc told me that I could never come back to his house. And if I wanted to see my momma, it would be on the streets because I was trying to set him up to be killed or some bullshit.

Bloccc gets on my nerves, and I hate the shit that he does, but I would never do no shit like that. I never discussed him with Sevino. Sevino didn't even know that he was my brother until just now and the reaction that I just got is exactly why I didn't want to tell him. This month has been one of the hardest that I ever had in my life. I start school in a few weeks, and I'm such a mess I don't even know how I'm going to pull it together to go.

With my tears blurring my vision, and my head held down, I made my way across the parking lot to Black's car. As I walked across the parking lot, cars were honking their horns at me for jaywalking, but I don't give a fuck. I never thought any of this was going to happen and that is part of the reason why I stayed away from Sevino. Ms. Matthews was so understanding and talked to me for over an hour, but I knew that Sevino wasn't goin' to handle me the same way. And he didn't.

"Bitch, is you crazy! These muthafuckas will run yo' ass over!" Black yelled as she pulled up on me, stopping traffic.

I slid into her car and just started crying even harder into my hands as Black held me.

"Nikia, stop crying, man," Black begged.

"Why the fuck is this happening? He wouldn't even hear me out, Blaccck!"

"SHNIKIA. SHNIKIA, WAKE UP, BABY," I thought I heard my mom saying, but I must be trippin'.

I rolled over and my momma was sitting on the edge of Black's bed.

"Bloccc bought you some stuff for school, and he opened yo' mail and got all the books that were required and recommended for your classes," my momma said as I wiped my eyes.

"He bought you over here?" I asked as I sat up.

"Yea, he's outside."

I start school tomorrow, but I still didn't have my books because I'm waiting for my financial aid to come through. I've been trying to hold on to all the money that I can because I'm not going to be able to work as much with school starting, and I've been giving Black money towards the bills. She didn't want it, but I'm not staying nowhere for free. I sat and talked to my momma for a few minutes. It's been a while since I saw her, and it seems like every time we talk on the phone, Bloccc comes in the house, and she has to go. I never paid it any mind because I know how my momma is when it comes to her precious son.

When Bloccc left me for dead in the parking lot, that was

the last time that I saw him. That was a week ago. He hasn't called, which I didn't expect him to. He told me that I was dead to him, so I'm confused why he is doing any of this. I looked briefly through the bags that my momma had put on the bed.

"Bloccc is getting me a place that's over there by where he lives. You can come stay with me," my momma suggested.

"Bloccc doesn't want me anywhere he pays the bills."

"Shnikia, look, baby. I don't know who this boy is that you been seeing, but you have to stay away from him. This has nothing to do with Bloccc. I'm telling you that you need to. You can't be with him."

"What?" I asked, pulling the cover off me, confused why is she coming at me 'bout Sevino.

"Shnikia, his family has taken so much away from us. And I don't care how much you care about him, you can't be with him!" My momma screamed as Black came in the room.

"Shnikia, why is you yelling at yo' momma?" Black asked.

"I'm not yelling at her," I said as my momma stormed out the room.

12

SEVINO

"You ready?" Auntie asked as she stood in the doorway of my room.

"As ready as I'm gon' get," I admitted as I looked at her through the mirror on my dresser and she walked away.

Today, I'm burying the person that gave birth to me. It's been a month since Trumaine and Mailman got hit. That day, when auntie was crying, she had gotten a letter saying that her sister was in a State hospital in Pueblo. She had been there for years and we never even knew. Her health was declining, and she requested for them to get in contact with auntie, and they did. Auntie begged me to go and see her, but I didn't. Her and Trumaine went and seen her a few times, but to be honest, I didn't have shit to say to her then or now. On the strength of Auntie is the only reason why I'm going today.

"Come on, baby. We need to go," Auntie said as I brushed my hair.

I ain't in no rush to get to the church, but Auntie wants to get there, so I snatched up my tool, and phone and made my way out. Shit been so fucked up, and with all this bullshit going on, all I been doing is being in the spot every chance I got, but I still ain't got nowhere. Trumaine fucked over that money and dope with the help of Wanii and whatever other bitch he been fuckin'.

"Sevino Matthews?" A woman asked as I walked on the porch.

"Who wants to know?" I spat.

"You've been served," The woman said and ran off the porch.

Auntie snatched the envelope that the woman gave me and pulled out the papers that were in it.

"What y'all doing? We need to go and who the fuck was that?" Trumaine asked as he jumped out the car.

"Oh My Go— Sevino baby, look at this," Auntie said, handing me some of the papers.

～

As THE PREACHER TALKED, that didn't know shit about the person in the urn, all I kept thinking about was them papers that's in my auntie's purse. How the fuck did she have a life insurance policy for two hundred thousand? She left it all to me. I'm the sole beneficiary of the policy. I didn't say shit to Trumaine about the money, but I called Mailman and told him to meet me here. The money isn't going to come today or tomorrow, but I need Mailman ready to put shit in motion as soon as it touches my hand.

Off the strength of our friendship, Mailman and his momma are sitting behind us. I just want to get the fuck out of here. I'm trying to be here for Auntie because she is taking this shit hard. She doesn't have no friends and doesn't talk to any of our family, so we're all that she's got. Trumaine keeps disappearing, and when he comes back over to where we are sittin', he's looking down at his phone, so I know it's some bullshit with Wanii. I don't have time to worry about his shit right now.

When his dumb ass came to me after he was down on his knuckles, I didn't have shit to say to him. And when it comes to that bitch, I still don't have shit to say.

Ain't nobody in here, but us and some ol' bitch that claims she's my god mom. I ain't never seen this bitch a day in my life. And she can save her stories from back in the day for her damn self because I don't want to hear 'em.

About thirty minutes passed, and the preacher finally wrapped this shit up.

Finally! Shit, I'm ready to go. They offered they condolences to us again and handed Auntie the flowers that somebody sent.

"Look, Thickems sent 'em," Auntie said. trying to show me the card. I shook my head and she put the card in the pocket on my dress shirt.

We made our way out the church and Mrs. Lewis, Mailman's momma, assured me that she would make sure that Auntie got home. Me and Mailman gotta go and shoot some moves. I don't where the fuck Trumaine is going, and I don't give a fuck.

Pop! Pop! Pop!

Shots rang out as soon as we made it outside, and then the car skirted down the block. I looked around, and me, Mailman and Trumaine are good. But when I looked down at my feet, Auntie and Mrs. Lewis are both stretched out with blood leaking from them. I rushed down to Auntie's side.

"Call the fucking ambulance!" I screamed.

Rat-a-tat-tat.

Pop! Pop! Pop! Pop!

As the bullets pierced through my skin, all I could think about was Auntie. I looked into her eyes as she struggled to try to say something and started choking on her own blood.

13

SHNIKIA

I've been up here every day for a month praying that Sevino would wake up, and every day when I come the nurse on duty tells me the same thing. That he isn't responding and still on life support. When Black told me that Sevino got shot coming out the funeral home, I already knew who was behind it. I guess that was my momma's way of saying that I was next if I came anywhere near him. She would never go against the grain and damn sure not against her baby Bloccc. I haven't seen or talked to my momma since that day. She's called, but I haven't answered. I don't have anything to say.

All I have been doing is going to class, work, and back up here to the hospital. I'm up here by myself right now doing my homework Ms. Matthews had to run some errands. My phone started ringing and it's Black.

"You hungry? You need anything? I'm finishing my last head right now," Black asked.

"Naw, I'm good," I said as my stomach started growlin'.

"Bitch, when is the last time you ate anything?"

"I ate earlier," I lied.

"Bitch, you gon' be hooked up to a fuckin' IV keep playing. Bloccc came over here earlier looking for you."

"Fuck him, I gotta go," I said, ending the call.

Mailman walked into the room and sat in the chair across the room, not saying anything. He does that every day. Mailman was always cool with me, but I know why I'm getting the cold shoulder now. Because of Bloccc, his momma is dead, and even though I had nothing to do with that, because of who I share blood with, I'm just as guilty in his eyes. I went back to doing my homework because right now, this is the only thing keeping me sane. I put my headphones, so I can get this shit done.

~

"Ma'am, ma'am, wake up. We need you to wait in the hallway," someone suggested, tapping my leg that was laid across Sevino, pushing it to the ground.

Sevino was moving and ripping the machines out of him. The nurses in the room called for back up and some people came rushing in the room, putting restraints on his arms.

"Ma'am, we really need you to wait outside," the woman said and ushered me out the room.

As she tried to console me, promising me that everything was going to be okay, I looked up, and Bloccc was leaning against the nurse's station staring at me. I tried to listen to everything that the nurse was saying but haven't taken my eyes off Bloccc while looking around to see if I see Mailman. I don't know if he left or not because when I fell asleep, he was still in the room. Checking the time on my watch, it's five o'clock in the morning, so I just prayed that he was far away from here.

"What type of bitch is by the nigga's bedside of the son of the nigga that killed her daddy?" Bloccc asked.

"What? What is you talking 'bout?" I asked as Bloccc walked over to me, now too damn close for comfort.

"You heard me," Bloccc spat.

"Yo' best bet is to take yo' ass over there to where Momma at and stay out the way because a bullet don't got nobody's name on it," Bloccc warned, kissing me on the top of my head and giving me chills.

Bloccc walked away as I looked down the hall at his back and watched his niggas one by one following behind him. I tried to call my momma. but she didn't answer, so I tried her again but still nothing. So, I went through my contacts and found the number of the only person that could tell me what the fuck Bloccc is talking about, get straight to the point and not hold shit back.

"Crybaby, what the fuck is wrong? Why you calling me so damn early in the morning? Is somebody dead shit?"

"No, grandad. I need to talk to you," I admitted as I paced around the hospital floor.

"Well, shit, call me after eight, hell," Grandad said and hung up on me.

Bloccc's attitude is just like my damn grandad's. Like he's his son and not grandson. My momma always told Bloccc how much alike they were, and Bloccc would get pissed until he grew up and decided that he wanted to take the spot that Grandad had. Me and my grandad aren't close and never have been. He refers to me as Crybaby and always has. He handles me as such every chance he gets.

A few hours passed, and the nurse came over to me in the lobby letting me know that I could go in to see Sevino now. Each step that I take towards the room was harder than the one before. It wasn't looking good, and I didn't think that he was going to ever wake up. My throat feels like it's closing, and my hands are shaking because I don't know how he is going to react.

Before the day he was shot, I called or texted him every other day and got no response. I talked to his Auntie here and there, but he wouldn't talk to me at all no matter how many times I tried. Mailman pulled me out of their spot just last week and told me that I needed to give him some space.

"Why are you here, man? Yo' people just tried to kill me, and you want to be here? Right now?" Sevino questioned as I walked in the room.

"Because I care. I know that you don't think that I do, but I do. I'm not a part of my brother's bullshit, and I can't control them or how they move. I'm here because this is where I want to be."

14

SEVINO

Looking at Shnikia, I don't know what the fuck to say. I don't have the strength to fight, and with all the blood I lost, they are looking for some now to try to piece it together, so I can get a blood transfusion in a few hours. As the doctor showed me x-ray's, I didn't know what none of that shit meant. All that mattered to me was I'm still here.

If I knew that Shnikia was Bloccc's sister when I walked into Black's, I would have left Trumaine there and kept it pushin'. Trumaine ain't quoted to the hood, he's affiliated because of me and Mailman, but he ain't got the same ties that we do. He would have fucked with Black and her if she would have let 'em.

"Who the fuck you been fuckin' with?" I asked because she the one disappeared on me with no explanation.

"Nobody, what type of bitch do you think I am?" Shnikia questioned.

"I didn't disappear, you did. And then you want to show up when shit start goin' bad."

"Look, I was just—"

"Lower yo' voice and put yo' hands down when you are talking to me," I spat, and she cleared her throat loud as hell.

"Like the fuck I was saying! I was dealing with a lot. I didn't talk to you about it because I didn't think you gave a fuck! My ex was killed on prom night, and at his funeral, all his bitches and babies came out. Shit, I felt guilty for fuckin' with you that's why I left yo' house that morning. I called you when me and my brother got into it because I didn't know who else to call. I never tell anybody about my brothers because they do so much bullshit, I never know who their enemies are."

"You willin' to go against all yo' people to fuck with me? Them yo' brothers."

"What do you know about Brian Richardson?" Shnikia asked as somebody knocked on the door.

"Come in," I said as Shnikia looked at me with fear all over her face.

"Girl, when is the last time you ate somethin' you lookin' like you on that shit?" Auntie said as she walked in and made me lose my breath.

I thought she was gone.

"Go and get something to eat and they need to check your blood to see if you're a match to be able to give Sevino what he needs so that he can come home," Auntie said as she came over to my bedside.

Shnikia made her way out the room, and Auntie sat down on my bed as I looked her over, not thinking that this shit is real. When I think back to the day that I got hit, I thought that she was gone before I blacked out. As she rubbed my hand, I knew that I wasn't dreaming, and she was here with me. We didn't say anything to each other for a few minutes. I think that we both were just trying to take it all in. I wiped the tears from her eyes as fast as they fell.

"Stop crying, we're good," I promised her as she put an envelope in my hand.

"Open it," she said as I wiped tears from her face.

I opened the envelope, and it had the check in it from the insurance policy minus the expenses for the funeral, I'm guessing by looking at the amount. The first thing I'm gon' do is get her out the hood, and right after, I'm going to get a brick.

SHNIKIA ROLLED her eyes at me as she came back in the room. I'm guessing because Yari just left out. Yari is Mailman's little sister. I don't want her ass and never will. She came up here for the same reason that Shnikia did, because she wanted to check on a nigga. Shnikia swears that we fuckin' or fucked before, but I never touched that bitch and never will. Mailman is like my brother; I wouldn't disrespect him like that.

"Let you tell it, I'm fuckin' the nurses, the phlebotomist, and every bitch that come in here, Shnikia. Don't start that shit. Not today," I spat.

They told me that I could leave yesterday, but I been up for five days, and I'm still in this bitch. Now it's because of my levels with my blood count. I just want to get the fuck out of here. This money is burning a hole in my damn pocket, and I need to get out, so I can put shit in motion to get Auntie straight. I signed it over to her for her to put it in the bank, so it would be cleared by the time I get out of here. It cleared yesterday and I'm still in this bitch.

"That bitch wants you. I don't give a fuck what you say," Shnikia spat.

"Shut up," I said as Mailman came in the room.

Shnikia looked at me and made her way out the room. I wasn't going to tell her to leave, and Mailman knows how we rockin' and how shit is going down.

"You talked to Trumaine?" I asked.

"The Teflon don? Naw, I ain't seen that nigga in a minute

either. I heard Wanii got a CPS case, so maybe that nigga at the house with his kids," Mailman said, shrugging his shoulders.

"How you holdin' up?"

"I'm alright," Mailman suggested but I knew better.

His momma was his everything. When his pops died when we were kids, she didn't miss a beat playing both roles. She never missed a basketball or football game for Blood. When some East side niggas jumped him and beat him with a base-ball bat, fucking up his knee because he was from the West side, he jumped headfirst into the game. With the limp and all.

"You heard anything?" I asked.

"Naw, but we both know who did it. You sure you can trust Shnikia?" Mailman questioned looking out the window.

"Yea, I can," I lied, not knowing if I can or not.

What the fuck am I getting myself into with this damn girl?

15

SHNIKIA

Looking over my shoulder, I made my way across the train tracks in front of my school. My brother meant that shit when he said a bullet doesn't have anybody's name on it, and I wouldn't be surprised if he had one of these bitches that's just here for a refund check watching me. Once I made it in the building, I sighed in relief that I made it another day to school.

Sevino should be getting out of the hospital tomorrow, and I'll be happy when he does because I'm so sick of being up there. Not to mention that I keep waking up having nightmares of Bloccc busting in the room and killing both of us. My grandad never called me back the other day, and I made a mental note to call him when I get out of class. I'm so damn happy this is my last class for the week, and I'm off from work this weekend.

"Nikia!" Somebody yelled from behind me, turning around it's this girl in my class named Myraina.

"If you ain't got no money, I don't know why you are calling my name," I said as she caught up to me.

"Damn, I can't get this one for now, and I'll pay you when I get paid?" Myraina asked.

"Quit fuckin' for free and you'd have twenty dollars," I said, shaking my head and sitting down at the table in the hallway, waiting for class to start.

"Mailman didn't have any change," Myraina whined and I shook my head.

"The price for pussy done went down, I see."

Ever since I can remember, Bloccc always told me as long as my pussy got wet, I should never be broke. As soon as he thought I was talking to niggas, he started saying that shit whenever I asked for anything. One by one, the bitches in my class who had twenty dollars came and went from my table with the homework that I did for them. Myraina was still sitting here with the sad puppy dog face. She knows me and has known me since I've been fuckin' with Vino. Considering the fact that our niggas our best friends.

"He, he hell. You better have my damn money on Tuesday," I said as I got up to make my way to class, handing her the homework.

"BABY GIRL, that dumb muthafucka ain't bought you a car?" I heard a familiar voice say as I waited for the light rail and texted Sevino.

"Grandad, what are you doing here?" I asked as I turned around. He looked me over and then finally hugged me.

"You called me waking me up out my damn sleep. Shit, it had to be important," Grandad said as he wrapped his arm around me, leading me to where his car must be.

"That was a week ago."

"Shit, I don't wake up before noon, and I don't come to the hood too often. Is it something you want to tell me, Cry baby?"

"You talked to Bloccc?"

"Naw, I ain't talked to that dumb muthafucka yet," Grandad said, opening the passenger side door on his Cadillac.

Grandad passed everything down to Bloccc when he was done with the game. Everything Bloccc knows about the game he learned from Grandad. The only reason why Bloccc got anything is because my dad isn't here. Grandad got in and started the car as E-40 blared through the speakers. Grandad turned down the music, so I know he is about to get back to questioning me.

"Are you good? Do you need anything?" Grandad asked as he pulled out the parking lot.

"I'm good. Block got all the books and stuff that I needed and me a new computer."

"I don't know about you staying over there with Black, I know she still hoeing."

"I'm hardly ever there, and I'm just saving up my money, so I can get my own place."

"So, what's this about you fuckin' with this nigga on the other side?"

I knew this was coming. Even though Steamboat, where Grandad lives with whatever bitch he lets stay the night, he still is a fuckin' gangsta. A real one, through and through. As I explained to grandad my side of the story, he took it all in and hasn't said anything or taken his eyes off the road. As we came into a traffic jam, my grandad hit the steering wheel as I spoke.

"Ain't this a bitch," Grandad spat, making me jump.

Bloccc doesn't scare me, but Grandad is something different.

"Cry baby, sit back and relax. Have I ever hit you?"

I took a deep breath and tried too, but his silence is scaring the fuck out of me. He ain't ever hit me but my aunts always talk they shit that they daddy never hit them, so a nigga never will. But I know how my grandpa feels about the Bloods.

"Do you know where yo' momma is from?"

"Naw, she never talks about her past. She always says it's behind her for a reason."

"She from the same hood that nigga you runnin' around with is. Look Crybaby, you ain't never been in this shit. But yo' ass was close enough to know that going over there was a no go. I can't tell you what to do, your grown. I ain't mad at cha. Do you love that nigga? You need to ask him what the history is with his family and ours. But I got another question, are you willing to choose him over Bloccc?"

The rest of the ride was silent, and the only thang that could be heard was E-40 and the wind. I don't know what to say. I love my brother, but he can't choose who I'm with. He can't tell me who I can love. I don't know if I love Sevino, but I do know that other than Bloccc, he's the only man that I can trust and know that he would never hurt me. After about thirty minutes, we pulled up to Black's apartment, and Grandad handed me some car keys.

"Don't have that nigga driving that car, Crybaby," Grandad said as he unlocked the doors to his car.

"You are giving me a car?" I asked confused because Grandad ain't the gift-giving type.

"You need a damn car, don't you? I'm on my way to the hood to talk to Bloccc. You need to talk to yo' momma. I don't like the bitch, but she still ya momma."

"Thank you, grandad," I said as he hugged me.

"Don't thank me. Become a damn nurse and don't be a bum like ya momma."

I shook my head and looked at Grandad before getting out the truck. Bloccc looks just like grandad. Grandad don't look nowhere near as old as his old ass is. As I hit the button on the keys Grandad gave me for the car, I see that it's his black on black Lexus. My phone started vibrating as I walked across the parking lot.

Bloccc: I'm giving you one more chance to go and stay with Momma and leave that slob nigga alone.

I put my phone in my purse and got in my new car while praying that I'm making the right decision.

16

SEVINO

"Sevino, I don't want to sit in the fucking house!" Shnikia yelled from upstairs.

I acted like I didn't hear her and finished cooking up the dope while Mailman caught me up with what's been going on. It's been two weeks since I been out the hospital and I've been in the streets every chance that I got since that money touched my hand. Shit, Shnikia been busy with school and shit, so that's all I been on. I prayed for this and I ain't gon' fuck it up. Shnikia and I got a spot in Aurora. It ain't much, but it's out the way. Auntie stays around the corner.

"So, what's the plan? It's been quiet, but you know that shit ain't gon' last for long, and we need to make some shit shake before them niggas do," Mailman demanded.

"I know, I know."

"Look, I don't give a fuck if you in love and shit with yo' bitch, but them niggas killed my momma."

Mailman has been patient and letting me get shit up and runnin' with his assistance and Trumaine, whenever he finds the fucking time, but I been putting shit in motion. Mailman playing it cool ain't even him. The nigga got his name for killing niggas and leaving them laying by they momma's mailbox. I know that this shit is about to go up, and once we make a move, ain't no going back.

"Damar! Are we going to do something or not?" Shnikia yelled as she came in the kitchen.

"Wassup, Nikia?" Mailman asked and Shnikia spoke back.

"Go take that fuckin' scarf off yo' head and get dressed," I said, and Shnikia smacked her lips and made her way out the kitchen.

"Tonight. Let me go and spend some time with Shnikia, and then after that, we gone ride," I said as Shnikia started calling my name.

~

"SHNIKIA, WE BEEN OUT ALL FUCKIN' day. I got to go and check on auntie and then we goin' to the fuckin house," I spat.

Shit, I'm tired, and I still got shit to do. We done been to Cherry Creek Mall, Park Meadows mall; we're leaving Ruth Chris now and she still ain't happy.

"I want to go to the movies. It's one that starts in twenty minutes, can we just go? It's right over there," Shnikia whined as I hit the locks on my new Blacked out Audi A8.

"Come on. Damn, Shnikia," I spat, giving in like I always do to her ass.

She kissed me on the cheek as I started up the car and pulled out into traffic. All this fuckin' traffic is irritating. Shnikia grabbed my free hand as I drove to the damn movies. To see a movie that I ain't even gon' watch. I know I'm gon' be fuckin' sleep. As we waited at the light on Speer and Broadway, a car pulled up on the side of us, with Boosie boomin' from the speakers. And I could barely hear it over Shnikia thinking she can sing in my ear.

"Girl, would you shut u—"

I attempted to say but was cut short by what I heard from the car on the side of me.

"Nigga, I don't give a fuck who in that bitch, send whoever in that bitch home!" A nigga spat.

"Nigga, you heard what OG said yo' little sister might be in there," a nigga whined.

"Fuck OG. You work for me, do yo' muthafuckin' job!"

Just as the light turned green, bullets started flying through my car, shattering the passenger side windows. I pulled out my tool and busted back as Shnikia hit the ground, pushing her seat back as far as it could go. I started bustin' back as people screamed, and Shnikia prayed, trying to get the fuck through this traffic.

"Fuck it," I spat. Driving down the middle of the lane with a red light ahead of me and oncoming traffic slowing down, I floored it.

As cars honked their horns and came real close to running into my shit, I made it through the light, and Bloccc and whoever was in the car were caught in the traffic and accident that I caused now. Once I was a few blocks away, I started slowing down, until I looked over and seen Shnikia's blood was splattered all over the passenger seat, and she wasn't moving.

"Go and do whatever it is that you need to do, Damar. I'm going to stay here with her," Auntie said as I stared off into space.

Shnikia was stable and she's just fine. The bullet that hit her went straight through, but she hasn't said one word to me since she's been up the past few hours. I been sitting in the lobby since she woke up and she wouldn't even acknowledge me. I went off on her ass until Auntie pushed and pulled me until I left the room.

"You need to give her some time," Auntie insisted.

I hear her, but I ain't tryin' to hear that shit. She can't blame me for this shit. Her brother was in that fuckin' car. I bet everything I have on that shit. If she wants to be mad at somebody, she needs to take that shit up with that crab ass nigga. I got up and made my way down the hallway to Shnikia's room.

"Look, if you want to be done, let's be done. I'm not 'bout to kiss yo' ass. You know what the fuck it was when you started back fuckin' with a nigga. I ain't keepin' no bitch that don't want to be kept!" I spat as I walked into the room with Shnikia and Black's eyes on me.

"Bitch?" Shnikia questioned.

"Yea, bitch. Because that's what the fuck you actin' like. So what the fuck is it going to be? I don't got all fuckin' night," I spat.

"Fuck you, Damar! I didn't ask for this shit!" Shnikia screamed with tears rolling down her face.

"Save them fuckin' tears. What the fuck is it gon' be?"

And she didn't say anything, so I made my way out and was met by Auntie at the door.

"You're wrong. You're dead ass wrong. Damar, that is not how I raised you. How the fuck do you think that girl feels? Her family has turned their backs on her because she wants to be with yo' black ass. And this is how you do her? Until you make shit right with Thickems, do not come to my house. Don't call me, and I don't want to see yo' face," Auntie warned, and I turned to walk away.

She already choosing her over me. Ain't this a bitch. We both knew what the fuck we were getting into when she decided to keep bringing her ass to the hospital and then left with me out that bitch and ain't went to far away since. My phone started vibrating and it's Mailman.

"Wassup?" I asked.

"I'm pulling up to the spot and they running through that bitch right now," Mailman said.

"Nigga, who? Some niggas? Then why the fuck are you on the phone with me, get them niggas," I spat.

"Blood, the fuckin' police," Mailman said, stopping me in my tracks in the middle of the hospital parking lot.

17

SHNIKIA

"Why the fuck wouldn't you call me, crybaby?" Grandad asked as soon as Dawn was out the room.

"You don't wake up 'til noon," I said, not wanting to talk to him or nobody else.

"Where the fuck is that nigga at? Who the fuck did this? Is he out handling it?" Grandad questioned.

"It was Bloccc," I admitted.

Before I hit the ground, I seen Bloccc's license plate pull up beside us. My heart started beating fast, and my palms started sweating, but I thought because Grandad had talked to him that we were good. We haven't had any issues with him. Bloccc hasn't sent any threats, and he even told me happy birthday and sent me roses and gifts to work last week. He always has bought me flowers and gifts on every special occasion, but I didn't expect that to continue, so I was just as confused as Nay was when our supervisor came into the break room with them. I knew they weren't from Sevino because the night before, he gave me his gifts when I wouldn't stop asking him what he got me.

"It was who?" Grandad asked me, trying to clarify what he already knew.

"Who you fuckin' this week?" Grandad turned, asking Black.

"What?" Black questioned, sitting up in the chair she was in.

"Grandad," I said because what the fuck does that have anything to do with anything.

"Crybaby, mind yo' muthafuckin' business. Now hoe, who you fuckin'? I need a favor."

"A favor?" Black questioned and had me looking at Grandad crazy.

"Hoe, I don't want none of that lil' pussy. I need a fuckin' favor," Grandad insisted, pulling out a rubber band and tossing it in Black's lap.

He had her attention as he whispered something to her. Black was making faces looking at me that would normally have me worried, but I don't give a fuck at this point. I can't believe Sevino came at me like that. The look in his eyes was just like the one I seen the last time we were at this fuckin' hospital. Grandad finished whispering to Black after a few minutes and came back over to my bedside,

"Crybaby, call yo' nigga," Grandad requested.

"What? For what?" I questioned.

"If I was going to kill him, I wouldn't be asking for you to call him. Girl, call the nigga before I act a fuckin' fool in this damn hospital!" Grandad screamed, handing me his phone, but I pulled out mine and call Sevino.

∼

I ROLLED OVER ready to push Black out of this fuckin' hospital bed. I don't know why the fuck she still here. I told her that I wanted to be by myself yesterday when she brought her ass here. And every time she leaves, she brings her ass back up here. As I laid eyes on Sevino instead of Black I was surprised. I don't know how he's feelin' so I don't know how the fuck I should feel about him being here.

"Why are you here?" I asked as I laid eyes on Sevino, who was just staring at me lookin' uncomfortable layin' next to me.

"I just went and met yo' grandad," Sevino said after a few minutes of just staring at me.

"And?"

"Look, Shnikia. My dad killed yours. Brian Richardson, right?" Sevino questioned, making my chest tight and all types of emotions are coming over me.

"What? Naw, how do you know that?" I asked confused.

"Yo' grandad just confirmed what Auntie told me when I was in the hospital."

"Why wouldn't you tell me that? "

"Would it had mattered? Would you had left?"

I didn't say anything because I didn't want to say the wrong thing. Being with Sevino gets harder every day. His money has grown, but that doesn't take away from the fact that I miss my family. I love Sevino, but all this got me questioning is it worth it. If what Sevino is saying is true, which my heart is telling me that it is, we were never supposed to be together. At this point, I'm questioning are we both living on borrowed time. Will it be worth it to stay together knowing that my brother isn't going to let up?

Me and Sevino sat and stared at each other until I couldn't take it anymore. I turned around and cried until I drifted back off to sleep.

∽

"WHERE IS SEVINO?" Black asked as I came downstairs with the shoes she wanted to borrow.

"I don't know. I haven't seen him since I got out the hospital. He's been here, but he comes and goes when I'm not here."

I been home for a week by myself, and Sevino not even bothering to call or check on me is what is fuckin' with me more than the pain from the hole the bullet left. Black was going out tonight but she on her own because the last thing that I want to do is go out and party. I'm just gon' cook and stay home. She'll either call me or show up over here in the morning to tell me everything that I missed.

"Just go and grab somethin', Nikia and come with me. Yo' grandad said that nothin' else is to move without his approval, so you don't have to worry about Bloccc," Black whined.

"Girl, I'm not going," I said for the final time.

I know what my grandad said, but I also know my brother. The only reason I been justifying staying here is because I was sick of being in Black's space. I also don't want to have to struggle paying high ass rent. And I'm not moving into a damn hole in the wall. Sevino clearly doesn't even want to see me, so I don't know why I'm holding on to staying here.

"Bitch, I'll be there when I leave the club. So be ready to make breakfast, bitch," Black insisted.

"Bitch, I'm not!" I said as I walked her to the door.

I made my way into the kitchen and started cooking. I put my food in the oven and went to lay on the couch, watch Tv and study until it's done. I ain't never talked to my grandad as much as I been talking to him lately. He calls everyday and don't be wantin' shit. I silenced his call because I damn sure don't want to hear his shit today. I got up to go and see if Black still had some wine over here. I haven't smoked since middle school and drinkin' ain't never really been my thing, but I need to relax. I ain't 'bout to turn into a dope fiend poppin' them pills that they gave me at the hospital, so I poured myself a glass of Rose and took a big gulp.

I just wish Sevino would come home when I'm here, so we

can talk. The fact that he been doing this shit is making me lose my fuckin' mind. Meanwhile, he just out there doing whatever the fuck he wants to do while I'm here waiting for him to come back. I don't know how much longer I'm going to be able to do this shit. I checked my steak in the oven, poured myself some more wine and made my way back to the living room.

A few hours passed, I ate and I'm getting sleepy. It's after one and Sevino still hasn't bothered to call or come home. I don't want to even get in our bed if Sevino isn't here, so I went upstairs to get a pillow and a blanket, so I can get comfortable on the couch. The alarm system alerted me that the front door was opening. I snatched up my stuff and tried to run downstairs, but the wine hit my ass hard and made my ass slow down.

"Bitch, just sit down here. I'll be right back," Sevino demanded to somebody as I made my way downstairs.

"Who the fuck is this bitch and why the fuck would you bring her to my fuckin' house!" I screamed and the bitch froze up.

"Yo' house? Naw baby, this ain't yours. I pay the bills here," Sevino spat, looking at me like I was a fuckin' joke.

"Bitch, because you pay the bills here, this ain't my fuckin' house? And bitch, why the fuck are you still in my mutha-fuckin' house!" I yelled and tried to get to the hoe Sevino done brought up in here, but he stopped me.

The bitch hit the door fast. Sevino grabbed both of my wrists and slammed me against the wall.

"Get the fuck off me!" I yelled.

"Calm the fuck down! If you don't like what I do in my house, than you can get the fuck out," Sevino spat as tears started rolling down my face.

"So, you just gon' bring a bitch in here where I lay my head? That's how you gon' do me?" I cried out with my hands still restrained.

"If you don't like the way I'm moving, there's the door," Sevino spat and let me go.

I slid down the wall and buried my face in my hands as I cried. I heard somebody yelling outside, but I don't give a fuck about them. I lifted my head long enough to see Sevino jog past me run upstairs and then right back out the front door. Then I heard him put his key in the door and lock it up as I cried my eyes out.

18

SEVINO

This is the last time I'm fuckin' with this bitch, Tahiri, that Black is draggin' up and down the street. At first, the shit was funny, but shit it's been ten minutes, and Black's crazy ass ain't lettin' up. I got tired of waiting for Tahiri, so I jumped in my car.

"You might want to go and check on yo' girl!" I yelled out the window to Black and pulled off.

That bitch can catch a cab I got shit to do. I don't have no more time to waste. I gotta go pick up this money from Mailman. Shnikia's grandad told me he was working on some shit and I haven't been able to find that nigga Bloccc, but I'm still keeping my head on a swivel and in the streets. Trumaine is locked up without bail and Wanii been in the fuckin' wind. I can't find that bitch. I know that all the money that was at they house, and the dope is with her wherever she's at.

I pulled up to Mailman's and Myraina in his front yard screaming at the top of her lungs with some damn boxers in her hand. This bitch is out her body. I told Mailman to leave her crazy ass alone, but he didn't listen. This bitch got a hold on this nigga that I will never understand.

"This is my shit! All this shit that you see. I don't give a fuck how long I'm gon' when I come back, it's still mine so all you bum ass bitches better stay the fuck away from Mailman! It's Mailman and My My til' this bitch blow!" Myraina screamed, recording herself and the fuckin' house.

"Go home, Myraina," I said as I walked up the stairs to the house.

"Nigga, I am home!" She screamed back.

"Why the fuck do you fuck with this crazy bitch?" I asked as Mailman opened the door to let me in.

"I love you, My!" Mailman screamed before shutting the door behind him fast.

"I love her crazy ass, but she be fuckin' trippin'. She swears it's a bitch in here. She in front of my house with my fuckin' draws in her hand. She all on Facebook posting that shit. She's crazy. But that's my baby."

"Then why yo' baby standing in the front yard?" I asked.

"Because that bitch is crazy, and I can't deal with that shit right now. Look, this is the money from the spot. Nigga, since Teflon been gone, I ain't been getting' no sleep trying to keep shit hummin'. And I got word that Wanii out here bad and CPS took the kids."

"What you mean, bad?"

As Mailman ran down to me what he heard about Wanii, I couldn't believe this bitch. She smoking dope, so that bitch probably damn near dead with what Trumaine had at her fuckin' house. But damn the kids. I tried to call Auntie, but she didn't answer. Which doesn't surprise me because she been staying true to her words. She ain't talked to me since the last time I seen her at the hospital. I left a message because this ain't about me; this is about the kids.

"Fuck! I gotta get them kids," I said.

"Nigga, you don't even like kids."

"I don't, but what the fuck I'm gon' do let em' stay in the system. If I get 'em, Auntie will handle 'em, and I'll just make sure they straight."

"We runnin' low on dope, we gon' need to call that nigga Truth."

～

"WHY THE FUCK is Crybaby missing school and work?" Shnikia's grandad asked as I sat down at the table he was sitting at in the Waffle house.

"Shit, I don't know," I admitted.

"I don't want to see my granddaughter end up like her mammy. Especially not over no fucking slob," Big Bloccc spat.

"What the fuck did you call me?" I asked, grippin' my tool.

"Nigga, you heard me. Jump. You won't make it to the exit, nigga."

I looked around and noticed five niggas at separate tables. They all nodded their heads at me, one by one, showing me their weapons.

"I'm not gon' tolerate no disrespect."

"And I'm not gon' allow you to turn my granddaughter into her momma. If I wanted you dead, I would have got you hit before yo' head left the pillow at Tahiri's this morning."

Shnikia hasn't seen me in two weeks. She calls and text every day, but I never answer. We just not meant to be and I can't keep putting her in harm's way. If this nigga knows where I laid my head at last night, then I'm sure that Bloccc does too, and I can't take no chances of nothin' else happening to her. She's a good girl and I owe her that much. I creep in while she's sleep and right back out. I didn't know she was fuckin' up in school.

Big Bloccc ran it all down to me about our meeting in a few

days with his people. I don't know how Mailman is going to take this, but if we want to keep going like we been going, it's time to have a sit down. I don't know if I should trust this shit, but right now, all I can do is take the chance.

19

SHNIKIA

"Grandad, I don't want to talk to Bloccc! I wanna go home and go to sleep. I have to work in the mornin'," I whined.

"I don't give a damn if Mary had a little lamb. Get yo' ass in the truck, Crybaby," Grandad insisted, holding open the door.

I rolled my eyes and slipped into his midnight blue BMW. I been seeing too much of Grandad lately, but he has been driving down here, taking me to and from school and work the past few days. I don't know how he knew I hadn't been going to school or work, but he wasn't having my shit. He kicked in the front door, triggering the alarm, and I been dealing with his shit ever since.

We rode in silence; Grandad and this damn jazz is getting' on my fuckin nerves. I got a fuckin' headache and I just want to go to bed. The direction we're goin', I know that we're headed to the hood. I know I'm not welcome there, but with Grandad being with me, I know I'll make it home alive. Bloccc is crazy but not as crazy as Big Bloccc. We pulled up to my momma's old house where clearly Bloccc done set up shop and Grandad threw the truck in park.

"If you love that nigga, you go in here and listen. Don't talk.

Listen. Show me that we got some of the same DNA," he said, got out the car and came over to open my door.

"Shit, Crybaby, you should be opening my door. Shit, I'm old," Grandad said as he wrapped his arm around me as we walked up the walkway.

～

"GRANDAD, I'M TIRED," I said, checking the time. It's almost two in the morning.

"Crybaby, shut up," Grandad demanded.

We been here for hours and Trigga and Grandad are playing two men spades because me and Bloccc opted out. What the fuck are we waiting for? Some of Bloccc's workers are here and Uncle Bone is here, I know on the strength of Grandad because he can't stand Bloccc. I have stuff to do in a few hours and Grandad is just having a good ole time, taking Trigga's money. Grandad's phone rang and he didn't say anything when he answered it. He ended the call, threw down his last card and got up, making his way to the front door.

"Nigga, you better have my money. Or that's yo' mutha-fuckin' ass," Grandad told Trigga.

Trigga whined and I'm supposedly the crybaby in the family. When I saw Sevino and Mailman walk in, I was confused. Sevino hasn't even looked over at me. Grandad told them to sit and for Trigga to get away from the table. Grandad didn't want Trigga anywhere near the streets, but Bloccc had other plans. Trigga, Bloccc, and me have the same dad, but Trigga has a different mom. I don't know much about her. Shit, Trigga been living with us since we were kids, so I don't think he knows much about her either. He calls my momma, Momma, so shit, I don't think he cares much about the woman that gave him life. Trigga is the baby, and he was definitely an outside baby, but Momma never treated him any different.

. . .

"THIS IS what I'm offering. You stay on yo' side and they'll stay on theirs. And we won't have no more problems. We'll let the past be the past, but if you come too far east, it ain't shit I can do for you... if you don't make it home," Grandad offered Sevino and Mailman.

"That ain't enough. This nigga killed my momma," Mailman spat as he lit his Black and Mild.

"I sent word to hit you niggas. I wasn't tryin' to hit yo' momma," Bloccc insisted.

"So what the fuck you want?" Grandad asked.

"The niggas dead who killed my momma," Mailman spat.

Grandad nodded his head.

Pop! Pop! Pop!

One by one, Bloccc shot down three of his workers and their brains splattered all over the living room walls.

"Anything else?" Grandad asked.

"Where's Wanii?" Sevino asked.

"Where she wanna be," Bloccc spat, like he gives a fuck about Wanii.

I didn't even know that he was fuckin' on her for the moment. Sevino nodded his head and stood up with Mailman following suit. As soon as they left out, I stood up because we should be leaving now.

"Sit down, Crybaby. Bring her ass in here," Grandad said, and Uncle Bone disappeared.

"If anything that's said in this room from here on out leaves this room, I will kill one of you muthafuckas," Grandad coldly spat, sending chills all over me.

"Crybaby, I love you to death, but I'll kill you," Grandad said in case I didn't get the message.

My mom came into the room slowly. I can tell she doesn't want to be here. Grandad doesn't hide the fact that he doesn't like her, and she always has seemed scared of him to me. She sat down on the couch with Trigga and me, but next to Trigga and just looked at me in disgust.

"I know y'all don't know this. I had no plans to ever tell y'all this, but uh ya momma used to be my bitch," Grandad said, catching all of our attention.

"I was never yo—" Momma attempted to say before Grandad shot her a look and shut her ass up.

"What the fuck is you talking about? Don't disrespect my momma like that, man," Bloccc growled.

"You might want to sit yo' big ass down and take some of that base out yo' voice. Because the bigger they is, the harder they fall. I ain't gon' fight yo' big ass, but I'll shoot you," Grandad spat.

I laid my head on Trigga's shoulder because it's about to be a long morning.

"Like the fuck I was saying. She was mine and Bloccc' is my son. And—"

"What the fuck?" Bloccc spat and jumped up, making the living room shake.

"Sit down and shut the fuck up. That's yo' problem; you talk too damn much. You get that from that bitch. I told that bitch to stop drinking while she was pregnant with you. Like the fuck I was saying. You got one more time to jump up, nigga and I'm gon' chop yo' big ass down!" Grandad screamed and Momma ran over to Bloccc's side.

"My son knew what the fuck it was. She wasn't my only bitch and I didn't really give a fuck about her. I was just fuckin' on my enemy's lil' sister," Grandad said, pausing to look over at me.

"That nigga you're dealing with daddy pulled the trigger to kill my son, but that was because he was paid to do it. I don't know how the fuck this makes y'all feel and I don't give a fuck. I didn't kill him over no bitch; she never meant nothin' to me. I had him killed because he was hard-headed. He talked too damn much. Was bringing too many young dumb niggas in. Like another muthafucka I know."

Grandad came over to me and kissed me on the top of my head, "Crybaby, you better take yo' ass to work tomorrow on time and to class on Thursday. I need a break from down here," Grandad said as he shook up with Trigga.

I nodded my head and Grandad made his way over to Bloccc and Momma, chuckling.

"You mad? You sad, nigga? I didn't play catch with you enough? I didn't help you with yo' homework, blame ya mammy! I gave you all this and nigga, just like God giveth, He can take it away. You remember that when you make yo' moves from here on out. Because nigga, I'm yo' God!" Grandad said and made his way out the door with Uncle Bone not far behind him.

"I'll see y'all on the next holiday and Crybaby, you cook because yo' momma never could do that. She thinks 'cuz she from the West side, she a pro at Mexican food and that shit was always nasty, hun Bone?" Grandad said before the door closed behind him. My phone buzzed and it was Sevino texting me, telling me to come outside.

When I got up, my momma turned up her nose at me, and Bloccc was just staring off into space as I walked out the front door.

We rode in silence to the house. I looked over and Shnikia was sleep. I heard everything that nigga said, but I don't trust Bloccc. I do know that they grandad used to run shit but that nigga Bloccc is a different type of nigga. I pulled up to the house and put my car in park and just watched Shnikia sleep so peacefully. I got love for Shnikia. She showed me love. Even when I was broke and all I could do was feed her and take her to work. Nikia never treated a nigga no different. When I came up, I blessed her and brought her with me.

I just don't know if, for the long run, if this shit is going to work.

"Are you leaving?" Shnikia asked as she rolled over and looked at me.

"I need to go and handle some shit."

"Can you please just stay?"

I didn't say anything, I killed the engine, got out the car, made my way around and Shnikia was still sitting in the car.

"Open my door!" Shnikia yelled.

"Girl, I'm not opening yo' door every time we get out the car."

"Open my door!"

"Shit," I spat and made my way in the house.

I made my way upstairs, and to the bathroom, so I can get in the shower. Mailman replaced my shower head and redid my bathroom, that I ain't even used yet. I turned on the shower, sat in the chair and looked around at Mailman's work. My nigga good with his hands; he is redoing his momma house on Custer. That bitch is cold. As I got in the shower, I can hear Shnikia stomping up the stairs and talking shit.

I don't give a fuck, I ain't opening her damn door every time she gets in and out the car. I ain't her fuckin' driver. She walked into the bathroom and sat on the toilet but hasn't said anything. She's just staring at a nigga.

I took off my clothes and got in the shower and Shnikia sat down watching my every move.

"Why the fuck you just staring at me? Come on," I said, and she just kept sitting there looking at me.

"Fuck it," I spat, and she started taking off her clothes.

∿

"You still not talking to me?" I asked as I walked into the kitchen where Auntie was sitting drinking her morning coffee.

"It took all that for you to talk to that girl and take yo' ass home?" Auntie questioned.

I didn't say nothin' because I'm still questioning if this shit is going to work.

"Umm, can you hear?"

"Right now she's content, but I know how much her brothers and Momma mean to her and having them in her life, I don't think that she can do that forever. Right now, she makes it seem like it ain't shit but ten years from now, is she still going to feel that way?"

"Are you willing to walk away and just leave her alone for good?"

"I think that's my only option. I don't want to be the reason she's miserable and unhappy. I care about her too much."

"You care about her, so who is this Tahiri girl?"

"Nobody," I spat, shruggin' my shoulders.

I don't give a fuck about Tahiri. She's a bitch that I slide on when I want and how I want. She doesn't ask no questions and don't require much. I thought that after Black beat her up I wouldn't see her again, but she was calling right after that asking could she see me. She's cool, but nothin' important for sure. I don't even know how the hell my aunt Dawn would know about her.

"How do you know about Tahiri?"

"Myraina came over here with Marcus earlier when he came to fix the stuff I asked you to fix," Auntie replied with her attitude evident.

"You mad? Auntie, I don't know how to fix that shit that's why I sent him over here. It got fixed, right?"

"I'm not mad at you. I'm mad at Wanii. I've called down to social services every day, and they keep saying they'll call me back, but they haven't. My grandkids should not be in the damn system, Damar!"

"I know. I been working on that. I'm still trying to get in contact with Wanii and her people, but I haven't been able to find her."

"Myraina said that Thickems' brother got her and she on that shit."

"What the fuck else did Myraina tell you? That bitch needs to be more worried about her own damn business while she's always trying to tell somebody else's."

I knew Wanii wasn't shit, we all did, but I did not think that she would start fucking Bloccc and get strung out. Whenever I hear anything about her, it's never good. From, the picture I seen of her that somebody made into a meme, she was all fucked up. She looks like a totally different person in a small ass amount of time. As my auntie started crying, I got up and made my way over to her and hugged her. The fucked-up thing is that with Wanii's scandalous ass family and the fucked-up system, who knows if we'll ever be able to bring Trumaine's kids home.

Trumaine was facing football numbers. Not only did they raid the spot, they had been following him for months and had him under surveillance doing all types of shit, including robbing Ericka and her nigga. He's not getting out; the judge already said he was a flight risk, so he can't even fight the case on his feet. Auntie insisted that she was fine after a few minutes of her crying. I keep waiting for them to come and get me, but let Trumaine's lawyer tell it, they aren't interested in me. Right now.

She made her way out the kitchen, so I washed my hands and started cooking because she said she was hungry. Who knows with her stressing about Trumaine when was the last time that she ate anything.

"Don't be burning nothin' in there!" Auntie yelled from the living room.

I ignored her. Shit, I know how to cook and finished cooking bacon, eggs, grits, toast, and cinnamon rolls. With Auntie talking shit from the living room the whole time. It took me about thirty minutes before everything was done, and I took Aunt Dawn a plate, so I can head out and handle some business.

"What's going on with you and Thickum's brother? Has she talked to her momma?"

"I don't know," I admitted.

21

SHNIKIA

"Why is you rushing me? Damn, I'm coming," I said as I snatched up my keys off the counter.

"Bitch, because I'm hungry, shit. You were supposed to be ready when I got here," Black said, pushing me towards the door.

"I don't want no fuckin' crabs anyway," I said as I locked the door.

I opened Black's car door and it's smoky as hell in this car.

"All you do is smoke weed," I said and we both started laughing.

"And slay hair, bitch. Don't forget that part!' Black said as I checked my hair in the mirror.

Black drove, and my mind was on me and Sevino. Everything has been good the past few days and I know that we promised to keep it real with each other. He's been coming home every night for the past week, but shit, I don't know what Bloccc is going to do next. I do know that he's going to do somethin', doe. He's never listened to grandad, ever. And with him finding out that he's his father, he's been on so much bullshit.

Black has told me so much hot shit that he's been doing.

Making niggas in Sevino's hood strip on the block, running they pockets and taking all they shit and making 'em move his work. That shit ain't sittin' well with Sevino and Mailman been on a rampage since they did that shit in front of his sister, to their cousin Lil' Mailman. As much as I don't' want this shit to come in between me and Sevino, somethin' is telling me that it is going to eventually.

"Come on, bitch," Black said as she got out the car and made her way into the Juicy Crab.

I got out and made my way in and the hostess walked me over to the table where Black and somebody else were.

"You ain't gon' speak?" My momma asked as I sat down and looked at Black.

"Bitch, really?"

"What, bitch? Y'all need to talk. This is yo' momma," Black spat and ordered a drink using her older sister's ID.

"Hi Momma," I said and texted Sevino back telling him to grab some stuff from the store for dinner tonight.

"How you been? You want to come home yet?" My momma asked and took a sip from her drink, not taking her eyes off me.

"I'm good."

"Give it a little while longer and you'll be back home," Momma insisted.

"Tell Shnikia about the house. Nikia, it's real nice," Black said, trying to stop me and Momma's staring contest.

"Bitch, how do you know?" I asked because she damn sure didn't tell me she been hanging out with my momma.

"I've been over there a few times," Black said and took a sip of this big ass drink the waitress just gave her.

"You been over there? For what?" I asked.

"Not to see me, to see yo' brother," my momma added.

The waitress came and took our food order and brought our calamari. I knew that she wasn't tryin' to see Trigga, so that lets me know that her dream finally came true and she's runnin' behind Bloccc. She knows firsthand how Bloccc moves and the fuck shit that he does when it comes to bitches, so I don't want to hear none of the bullshit, and she already knows that. That's why she hasn't said anything, but that would explain the fuckin' new thirty-inch tracks, the watch glistening on her wrist and the new Moschino bag she has. Bloccc very rarely pays for the pussy, but if he wants it and it's comin' from a bitch he respects, he'll spend some money on it and put in some work.

"So, what's been goin' on?" My momma asked as the waitress bought out our food.

"Work and school."

"Work and school, hun? What else has been going on?"

"You taught me you don't talk out yo' house," I said and started eating my shrimp and fries.

Black could have at least told me that she was going to be here. This shit is awkward as hell, and as we sat and ate every time my momma talks, it's about some shit that's going on in the hood. She was watching what she says, not giving no names and not implicating Bloccc in anything. She has always been overprotective when it comes to Bloccc, and considering the situation, I know now why she goes so hard and rides for Bloccc the way she does.

After about thirty minutes, we finished eating and made our way out. I seen Bloccc in the parking lot waiting for Momma. He nodded his head when we made eye contact, and I threw up my hand, hugged Momma, and snatched Black's keys making my way to her car. She made her way over to Bloccc, of course, but what surprised me is that he got out the car and hugged her.

I've never seen him do that for no bitch. But I can remember one day him snatchin' me up when I leaned in Rayvon's car when he pulled up in front of our house. He didn't play that shit and told me that a real nigga would get out the car and not have you leanin' in the car like I was tryin' to sell pussy. He cussed me out so damn bad and was ready to kill Rayvon that day.

~

"Have a good night. I'll see y'all on Monday," I said as I made my way out the break room at work.

I'm so damn tired, and I still need to go home and do some homework. I have class in the morning, and I just want to go home and get in my bed. When I walked out to my car, I seen Bloccc in the parking lot talking' to Nay, and if Monica comes out here and sees this shit, it's goin' to break her lil' heart. I shook my head as I got in my car. I started up my car and looked in my mirror and met eyes with Bloccc's second in command, Soda.

"Cut off the car," Soda spat.

"I'm not cuttin' off shit. Get the fuck out my car," I spat, not taking my eyes off of him.

"I don't give a fuck about you. I don't give a fuck about yo' grandad and whatever the fuck he says. That slob ass nigga you fuckin' took from me and I want what's mine," Soda said, putting me in the headlock and pressin' his gun to my head.

"What do you want?" I asked with tears coming down my face.

"Call that Slob," Soda spat.

22

SEVINO

"Bitch, shut up," I spat as Tahiri whined about Shnikia calling me.

"Wassup, baby?" I asked as I answered.

"This ain't yo' muthafuckin' baby. I don't give a fuck 'bout whatever you and Bloccc done agreed to, I want my muthafuckin' money," a nigga spat.

"Where is Shnikia? And who the fuck is this?" I spat.

"Soda, Slob. Bring my money plus interest from what Mailman took from my spot, and you can have Shnikia. I need two hundred thousand. We'll be at Civic City Park. You got 'til midnight," Soda spat and ended the call.

"Get out," I spat as I pulled over on the corner of Colfax and Peoria.

"Get out? What the fuck I'm supposed to do, walk?" Tahiri questioned.

I hit the locks and reached over, opening the door and pushed her ass out. As I sped off the door closed on, its own. I have to get to Mailman and get this fuckin' money together, so I can go get Shnikia. My phone started ringing and it's Tahiri, but I sent her ass to voicemail and called Mailman.

I went through every light that I passed, whether it was my time to go or not. I didn't know shit about Mailman taking no money from them. Shit, our money has been good, it's no reason that he would be hungry and willing to start some bull-shit over some money. He doin' better than good and right now isn't the time to be greedy. I know that Soda is Bloccc's main man so just like that, the truce is over. Once I made it to Mail-man's, I ran in the house and ignored Myraina's bipolar ass sitting in the middle of the floor crying.

"Why the fuck wouldn't you tell me that you been hittin' they spots?" I asked as I walked in the kitchen where Mailman was cooking dinner.

"For what, so you could stop me?"

"Soda got Shnikia and he want two hundred thousand by midnight."

Mailman turned to face me.

"What happened to the truce?"

"Nigga, I'm guessing you robbing them got something to do with it. I need you to give me the hundred that you took. Look, I know that him killin' them niggas ain't gone bring yo' momma back and I can't even say that I know how the fuck you feelin' because I ain't never had no momma, but nigga, this is my girl. I can't let nothin' happen to her in behind some shit that don't even got nothin' to do with her," I spat as Mailman opened the freezer and started pulling the money out of empty food boxes.

"You right; you don't know how the fuck I feel," Mailman said as he dropped the last stack on the kitchen table.

I'll finish talkin' to him later, but right now I have to get to my house to pick up this money and then downtown to the park so I can get Shnikia. It's about the money, so I don't think that Soda would fuck with her or do nothin' to her, but shit, you never know what a muthafucka would do until they do it. It took me about an hour to run to the house, get the rest of the money and make it downtown to the park. I'm sittin' next to a homeless man on a bench lookin' around for Soda.

"You got my money?" Someone said from behind me.

Then Soda walked in front of me, I looked around for Bloccc because I never knew them to make these type of moves without each other.

"What you lookin' for? Bloccc?" Soda asked.

"Yup," I replied.

"This ain't got shit to do with Bloccc. Yo' nigga took my shit and I'm not lettin' shit slide. Big Bloccc ain't runnin' shit this way." I tossed him the backpack with the money in it. He looked through it, thumbed through the money and zipped the backpack back up. Then turned to walk away.

"Where is Shnikia?" I asked through clenched teeth, gripping my tool.

"Oh damn. You want her, hun? Damn, let me think for a minute. Where the fuck is she at?" Soda said, pissin' me off.

"Damn, where did I put her? Slob ass nigga, she over there in her car," Soda said, laughing and pointing.

I took off running before he could say anything else. When I got to the car, Shnikia was in her bra and her work shirt was stuffed in her mouth hogtied. Her hands were tied to the stirring wheel. I ripped the hogtie that was damn near choking her out, and her once muffled cries blared out. Once I got her untied from the steering wheel, she wrapped her arms around my neck and cried into my shoulder.

"Why is this happening?" Shnikia cried out.

23

SHNIKIA

Today has been a long day. I stepped outside to get some air, and Bloccc is in the parking lot, but none of his bitches ain't out here with him. That surprised me, but I don't care.

"Nikia!" Bloccc called out.

I threw my hand up because I don't have nothin' else to say.

"Girl, come here!" He spat.

I made my way over to his car and got in, leaving the door open.

"What the fuck I do to you?" He asked.

"Wassup, Bloccc?"

"I just wanted to check on you. I know what today is, and even though you fucking with that nigga, I know you," Bloccc said in between doing somethin' on his phone.

"I'm good," I lied.

"You need anything?"

"Naw."

Today is Rayvon's birthday and it's been kind of hard for me. I had to log off Facebook because I didn't want to see the posts. It's been two weeks since Soda was in my backseat and held me for ransom. I keep waiting for some more bullshit to happen, but so far nothin'. But Bloccc showing up here has me thinkin' some more bullshit is about to happen. I never had to question Bloccc having my back until I got with Sevino, but now I know no matter what he sees me as an enemy.

"Why ain't you called Momma or been to see her?" Bloccc asked.

"Momma don't want to talk to me or see me, Bloccc."

"This shit don't got nothin' to do with her."

"Did you have Soda snatch me up?"

"What?"

"What the fuck is you talkin' about? Soda did somethin' to you?" Bloccc asked, grabbin' my face, turnin' it towards him.

I snatched away because I don't know if I can believe him or not. I told him everything, and as he took it all in, I could see his mind racing. He started tappin' the steering wheel.

"On Momma, I didn't have nothin' to do with that shit," Bloccc spat. I looked up and Sevino was in front of us leaning against his car.

"Call me if you need anything," Bloccc said and started up his car.

I didn't say anything; I just got out the car. He hasn't taken his eyes off Sevino and I don't want no bullshit to go down at my job.

"Why the fuck was you in the car with that nigga?" Sevino spat, pushin' me back as I walked up on him, tryin' to hug him.

"What? You actin' like I'm tryin' to get with some nigga in the streets. That's my fuckin' brother," I replied, crossing my arms over my chest.

"That's my fuckin' enemy, Shnikia!" Sevino spat.

"And that's still my brother."

"Stay the fuck away from him," Sevino said and reached in his car, handing me a Chic-fil-a bag and a drink.

"I'm surprised to see you, bitch. You been actin' funny," Black said, counting her money from the girl that just got out of her chair.

"I needed a break from Sevino," I admitted.

When I got out of work, I came to Black's. I don't know if he's at home or not but I don't want to argue about him and Bloccc's shit tonight. When he left my job, he was mad as hell, but I'm still mad. He can't tell me to stay away from my brother. I would never cross him, and at this point, I feel like he's questioning my loyalty to him. I blew up my family to be with him and that shit doesn't seem to matter. My phone started ringing as Black's client went out the front door.

"Hello," I spat as I answered Sevino's call.

"Where the fuck is you at?" Sevino spat.

"Where the fuck is you at?" I questioned.

"Shnikia, I don't have time to play with you. My big homie just got killed; where the fuck is you at?" Sevino yelled.

"I'm at Black's. Where are you?"

Click.

"I'm so sick of this fuckin' nigga!" I screamed.

"Umm, bitch, calm down. What the fuck is goin on?" Black asked as she came in the kitchen.

"I went through Sevino's phone last night."

"When you go lookin' for somethin', you're goin' to find it," Black said and leaned up against the counter, lighting her blunt.

"I didn't tell him. I didn't say nothin' to him. Black, I'm giving up everything to be with this nigga, and he out here fuckin' other bitches. He got me out here lookin' stupid as fuck."

"You know that you can always stay here."

24

SEVINO

"Look at this, baby. Ain't she cute?" Shnikia asked as we laid on the couch and she showed me some baby on her phone.

"Unn hun. Why you talkin' 'bout babies so much? You pregnant?" I asked, half lookin' at the picture off Facebook on her phone.

"No, but don't you want kids?"

"Naw, I don't want no damn kids," I said, and she leaned off me, staring at me.

"What you mean, you don't want kids?"

"Exactly what I said."

"Well, I do."

"Better go and get a puppy," I said. She got off the couch and stormed upstairs.

My phone started ringing and its aunt Dawn. I hope she got some good news about the kids, but the way shit been goin', I doubt it. Trumaine was taking his case to trial. They offered him a deal, but with that shit, he'll never come home. I just got him a new lawyer. It's been months and that last one hadn't done shit. Auntie caught me up with what the lady from social services said and it's like the kids are missing, and they actin' like they can't find them. They ain't doin' shit to find them as far as I'm concerned.

"Anyways, where's Thickums? Y'all should come over."

"Where the fuck is you going?" I asked as Shnikia stormed down the stairs with a duffle bag packed to the top with shit comin' out of it.

"The fuck away from you," Shnikia spat and made her way out the door.

I told Auntie I would call her back and made my way outside.

"What the fuck is you trippin' for, because I don't want no kids? Look, Shniki—"

"You look, I done gave up everything to be with you! And you out here fuckin' bitches and doin' whatever the fuck you want to do. So, I'm gon' do what the fuck I want to do!" Shnikia screamed.

"What the fuck is you talkin' bout? I ain't out here fuckin' no bitches," I lied.

"Oh, you not? Nigga, do I look stupid to you? What the fuck is this? What the fuck is this?" Shnikia asked, flippin' through pictures in her phone that she took of messages in my phone.

"What the fuck is you doing goin' through my phone?"

"You know what? Nigga, fuck you and yo' phone!" Shnikia spat, snatching away from me and jumpin' in her car.

From the date that was on the top, she took them a week ago and hadn't said shit. I made my way back in the house. I'm not chasing her ass today. I made my way upstairs, went into the bathroom and it's a fuckin' pregnancy test on the counter. I picked it up and it's positive.

∿

"WHERE YOU GOIN'?" Mailman asked Myraina as she came through the kitchen holding her son, Marshawn.

It's crazy that ain't even that nigga seed and he looks just like Mailman. He even got Mailman's name. When he met Myraina crazy ass, her son was probably like two and you can't tell that nigga that lil' nigga ain't his. I'm all for steppin' up for shorty but this crazy bitch Myraina, I don't see how the fuck he deals with her ass. She makes me want to drink and I don't even fuckin' drink. Mailman made his way out the kitchen with them.

It's been damn near two weeks and Shnikia ain't been home. I called her phone for a few days, and she ended up changing her fuckin' number. I done been to her job, up to the school, to Black's and she ain't never nowhere around. I'm at the point where I'm just ready to let her ass go. I'm not with all this chasing shit and I'm not about to play these games with her ass. She can go on back to her momma's.

"Ride with me real quick," Mailman said as he came back in the kitchen snatchin' up his keys.

I ain't even been tryin' to be at the house since Shnikia ain't there. I been staying at Aunt Dawn's, taking cat naps and getting' right back to the money. The only time I go home is to change clothes and check on the house. Auntie be lonely and shit, so she be wanting me at the house with her, so it's been working.

"Where the fuck we goin' Blood?" I asked because we definitely leaving the West side.

"I gotta go and handle somethin'. I just need you to watch the door and don't let nobody in that bitch!" Mailman said in between taking pulls from his blunt.

"I got you," I said.

I don't even need to know what the fuck is on the floor. Mailman had my back through so much shit and didn't switch up even when I thought he might. I know that he was against me being with Shnikia, and he had good reason, but his loyalty never changed. He never even spoke on it. After about twenty minutes, we made it to the same apartments that Black lives in. The look in Mailman's eyes I've seen before, but not since we left out of the meeting with Shnikia's people. We been strictly on gettin' money shit and nothing else.

Mailman pulled up a few apartments down from Black's and pulled in the no parking, fire zone and threw on the flashers. It's a U-Haul and some people moving shit in right behind us. As I got out, I see Black's car, but I don't see Shnikia's. We made our way to the apartment, and Mailman wasted no time kicking the door right between the lock and the door frame, busting it right down. I just posted up outside the door like he requested.

"What the fuck, Shnikia? Why wouldn't you call me? Where are you at?" Black yelled as she fumbled through her purse coming out her door.

"Alright, Alright. I'm on my way," Black said.

"Ayye, Black!" I called out, while listening to Mailman kickin' somebody's ass.

Mailman was talkin' shit and whoever ass he's kickin' is begging for him to stop. All I can hear besides Black talking is shit breaking and falling over.

"What?" Black finally responded.

"What's goin' on with Shnikia?" I asked.

"Nigga, if you cared, then you wouldn't still be out here fuckin' random bitches!" Black yelled.

"Black, for real, what the fuck is goin' on/ She left me; I didn't leave her," I said, checkin' my surroundings and keeping an eye on the door as I walked closer to the curb.

"You didn't give her no other choice. I've watched her go from being sweet and innocent to turnin' into this mad crazy bitch all behind you," Black spat.

"Black, what the fuck is goin' on?" I asked, and Black ended her call with Shnikia, coming over to where I'm standing.

As Black ran shit down to me with a fuckin' attitude like

she's my bitch, I don't know how to feel about the shit I'm hearing. I ain't feelin' the way that Black is feeling and that would explain why she stormed off. I made my way back to the apartment door where Mailman is, and I peeked in. Myraina's real baby daddy was damn near dead. Mailman came out, ripped off the Black T-shirt that was covered in that nigga's blood and made his way to the car.

Mailman and I discussed Myraina's crazy ass all the time, but I don't know much about that nigga Ray. I only know his name because I heard somebody else say who Myraina used to fuck with. As far as Blood is concerned, that lil boy is his and if anybody even tries to question it, they gon' be fucked up like Ray. I've seen a few bitches and niggas fucked up sayin' any damn thing about him not being that lil' boy's dad.

"I need to go to the hospital," I said as Mailman skirted out the parking lot.

"Which one?" Mailman asked.

"University," I said in between lightin' my blunt.

25

SHNIKIA

"Bitch, I'm good," I said as Black cried into my shoulder.

I cried when I got the news that I was having a miscarriage. I cried even harder when they told me that they had to remove my fallopian tubes, but when they told me that I would never be able to have kids naturally, I felt my heart break. That was exactly a week after I left Sevino. Imagine going through that type of shit alone. I was too embarrassed and broken to even call Black. I couldn't call my momma and damn sure not my brothers. Trigga has tried to stay neutral throughout the shit with me and Bloccc, but this gang shit is in our blood and ain't no escaping it.

I called Black now because I need somebody to drive me home. With the medicine I'm on there is no way that I can drive myself. I was in so much pain when I went to my doctor to just confirm that I was really pregnant, they told me that I needed to come to the emergency room. When my regular doctor told me from the pain and spotting I was experiencing, he thought I was having a miscarriage, I didn't want to believe it. When I got up here and they found out that the baby was in my tubes, I was devastated. Yea, I want to be a nurse and work with children, but I also have always wanted to be a mother and have a family.

"Bitch, shut up. Quit cryin' before you make me start cryin' again. Why the fuck are you so damn emotional? What the fuck is wrong with you?" I asked as Black got off the bed to get some tissue.

"I'm still mad at yo' ass for not calling me, Shnikia. I don't give a fuck what it is, you should be able to tell me everything. Bitch, we tell each other everything and always have. I don't give a fuck what it is. Bitch, you call me to tell me that the nail shop didn't have yo' color!" Black complained.

"I know, Black, but I didn't want to tell nobody what the fuck was goin' on."

"Shnikia, I don't want to hear that shit," Black spat in between blowing her nose.

We sat and talked for about an hour and my stomach started growlin' while I looked at the now cold food that was on a tray on the side of me. Black looked over at me and rolled her eyes. I thought that they would have let me go by now. I was supposed to be discharged, but now they want me to stay another night because of test results they got back.

"Bitch, what do you want to eat?" Black asked after a few minutes with an attitude.

"Chic-fil-a," I replied and Black got up, snatchin' up her purse and made her way out the room.

I heard somebody tap lightly on the room door and I just prepared myself for one of the nurses to come take my vitals for the millionth time. I looked up and it wasn't a nurse or doctor. It was Sevino. He didn't say anything but had flowers and balloons that say I'm sorry. He's the last person that I want to see right now.

How the fuck did he know I was here?

"Why the fuck are you here? You can take them funky ass

flowers, balloons and give 'em to yo' bitch Tahiri," I spat as he tried to hand me the flowers but I knocked 'em to the ground.

"I know that your mad and you got the right to be, but you should have fuckin' called me," Sevino said, sitting the balloons down.

"Called you for what? Did you forget we are done! We don't have shit to discuss! I didn't call you because I didn't want to see your fuckin' face! You made it clear where the fuck we stand! Ever since you got that money, you changed. When you were barely able to re-up, I was there! Now all you care about is money, cars, and shit! You don't give a fuck about me and probably never did!" I screamed with tears streaming down my face.

"I didn't fuckin' change. I'm still the same nigga you met," Sevino spat.

"If you can't even be real with me, then get the fuck out!" I cried out.

Knock, knock, knock.

"Ms. Richardson, are you okay?" My nurse, Ms. Lena, asked as she walked in my room.

"I'm okay."

"Are you sure?"

"Bitch, she said she's okay!" Sevino spat.

I wiped my tears away, trying to convince Ms. Lena that I was good, but she wasn't buying it because she hasn't left the room. Looking at Ms. Lena, you would think that she was some old Korean lady, but Ms. Lena plays no games. If you could hear the way she talks to her co-workers when they fuck up, then you would know she's not to be fucked with. Her being here every day is the only thing that has kept me going. She wouldn't let me mope around; she comes in here every day opening the blinds and playing music on her phone.

"I'll be okay," I said, trying to get Ms. Lena out the room because I can see how mad Sevino was getting with her presence.

Ms. Lena looked at me long and hard and mugged the fuck out of Sevino, as he jumped out his seat ready to move her ass.

"I wish the fuck you would," Ms. Lena spat and turned to face Sevino. Then made her way out the room.

"You don't need to be here. Pretending to be concerned," I said, breaking the awkward silence that lingered in the room.

"I'm here because I love you, Shnikia. You know how much money I could be making."

"Then get the fuck out, go and make some money."

I pulled the cover over me and turned away, so I didn't have to look at Sevino anymore. I never thought that I would end up in this situation. When I envisioned my future, I didn't see none of this happening. I keep waiting to hear the door close behind him, but I never heard it. As my tears flowed, I just wanted him to hug me and comfort me, but at least a few minutes have passed, and I still don't feel his touch, smell his scent or feel the security that he is going to be here for me, while I deal with this.

I started tryin' to force myself to go to sleep, but my mind was racing. Why can't he love me the way that I want to be loved? Why is he even here, if he's not willing to change? What does he see in Tahiri that he doesn't see in me? As I tried to turn my mind off, I felt Sevino get into the hospital bed with me. He hugged me tight and I started to let it all out. I know that I'm not going to get over this overnight, but I still want to know if Sevino is goin' to ride this shit out with me?

"I KNOW THAT YOU WITH YO' man, but I just want to make sure that you're good and don't need anything. Do you want me to go and pick up your prescription?" Black asked as we walked out the hospital.

"He's not my man. I don't know what the fuck we are

doing," I admitted, and Sevino snatched my arm as soon as the words left my mouth.

"Let me fuckin' go," I spat, snatching away from him.

I led the way to Sevino's car and he was right by my side. Yea, he held me all night and only left to go and meet Mailman in the parking lot because he dropped off his car- he claims. Who the fuck knows who came up to the hospital. It could have been that bitch Tahiri for all that I know. I'm sick of tryin' to make him open up and talk to me. I don't even know why the fuck I'm going home with him. I want to work things out, but damn what the fuck am I supposed to do?

"Look, Sevino, if you can't fuckin' talk to me and make some fuckin' changes. I might as well just go with Black!" I yelled and looked over at Black leaning against her car.

"Shnikia, lower your fuckin' voice when you're talking to me!" Sevino demanded, pushing me into the passenger side door of his car.

"Look, I fuckin' love you! I don't know how many fuckin' times you want me to tell you that shit! I don't give a fuck about no bitch other than yo—"

"Nigga, I ain't no fuckin' bitch!" I yelled, cutting him off while we still are chest to chest.

"Shut the fuck up and listen! Whatever the fuck we gotta do to make this shit work, I'm ready to get it done! We done been through too much and stood tall to let anything come in between what the fuck we got! You right, you were there for a nigga when I didn't have shit, and that's why I fuckin' love you!

I don't want nobody else by my side. I don't want to wake up to nobody else in my bed! I don't want nobody else in my fuckin' kitchen! I don't want nobody else callin' me whining about they fuckin' hair and nails," Sevino said, now grippin' my ass as I wrapped my arms around his neck.

"I want you! Fuck it, you want a baby, we can try again," Sevino said, making me start crying into his chest.

"What's wrong? Why is you crying now?" Sevino asked.

"I can't have a baby. I can't have any more kids," I said with tears streaming down my face.

As Sevino consoled me, I couldn't help but still feel the pain in my chest. Even with all that he just said, I don't know if this hurt will ever go away. A few minutes passed and no words were exchanged between us. I know that he's sick of hearing me cry, but he hasn't said anything.

"She's good. You can go home. She's not coming with you," Sevino spat to Black.

"Muthafucka, you don't know what she's goin' to do!" Black yelled back.

"Let's just go," I said, breaking our embrace.

Sevino flicked off Black.

"I'll call you when I get home," I said and waited for Sevino to open my door.

He looked at me crazy, but he opened the fuckin' door. I got in. I tried to get comfortable but I can't. I just want to go home and get in my own bed. I don't give a fuck what Sevino says and how much money he's missing out on, he's not going anywhere. Sevino went back and forth with Black for a few more seconds and then got in the car.

We didn't say anything to each other. He just held my hand as he drove with his free hand. If this is really going to work, we are both going to have to put in work to get it right. I feel that the worst has to be behind us, so if we made it through that, than anything else shouldn't be an issue. I know that it is not going to be easy. My fucked-up relationship with my family is still weighing heavy on my heart.

Me and Bloccc have always bumped heads, but whenever I needed him, he was always there. Talking shit, but he was there. I don't know how Sevino is going to feel about it, but I want to try to get back cool with my family. Bloccc cares too much about the hood, he would never fuck that up to get at

Sevino now with the way Grandad acted when he found out what Soda did. Shit, Sevino isn't on his level yet and Bloccc knows that. He studies niggas and how they move and what position they hold especially his enemies.

After about ten minutes, we made it to the house and somebody's car was in the driveway. I can't see who it is.

"Sevino, I really want to try to make this work, but you have to be willing to talk to me," I said as he killed the engine.

"Alright," Sevino replied.

"Don't just say alright to get me to shut up, Sevino!"

"I'm not. Whatever the fuck we have to do, I'm gon' put in the work," Sevino assured me.

"Who the fuck is that in the driveway?" I asked, looking away.

"I don't know," Sevino said, getting out the car and making his way to open my door.

"Get the fuck out my driveway!" Sevino spat, helping me out the car.

"Nigga, I'm not going nowhere. For the next eighteen years, you stuck with me, nigga!" The bitch yelled as she got out the car.

"Who the fuck is this bitch?" I questioned because I've never seen her before.

"This bitch, I used to fuck. Lay," Sevino spat.

I snatched away from Sevino and leaned against the car. Looking up in the sky just tryin' to figure out why the fuck was all this happening. I can tell from the way that Sevino is looking at me but glancing over at Lay, he wants to comfort me, but he also wants to address Lay. *What the fuck have I gotten myself into fuckin' with this nigga?* I thought as I took off on Lay because she had gotten too close to me.

EPILOGUE

SHNIKIA

Three years later...

"Hurry up, Shnikia! Before I leave yo' ass!" Sevino yelled from downstairs.

"I'm gon' leave yo' ass!" Sevino yelled out as I heard the front door slam.

He can just go and I'll meet him there. Who threatens to leave somebody on their graduation day? Only this nigga, for sure. We've been through so much shit and I didn't think that we would ever get to this place. Don't get me wrong; it's still days that I feel like I want to choke him the fuck out, but he has made a lot of changes. I just don't want to argue today, so hopefully, he doesn't piss me off.

I made my way downstairs strugglin' in these damn heels. I didn't want to wear heels, but I let Black's ass talk me into it. Hopefully, I don't end up walking across the stage in the flip flops I have in my purse because this shit just ain't me. I'm a tennis shoe or flats type of girl. Heels are cute and all, but I only wear them for days like today. When I made it outside, Sevino was leaning against his car holding Lil' Vino.

When Lay showed up at the house screaming to the world that she was carrying lil' Sevino, I didn't think that me and Sevino would have made it here today. I damn sure didn't think that I would be raising his child by somebody else. It took a lot for me to even talk to Sevino after that day. He stopped me from jumpin' on Lay and picked me up kicking, screamin' and took me in the house. I contemplated leaving and did, but I came back.

"You look good," Sevino said, lickin' his lips.

"I know," I said, waiting for him to open my door.

"Get in the damn car," he said, swingin' open my door and then waiting for me to struggle taking four steps to get into the car.

Sevino closed the door behind me and then got Lil' Vino in the car. Sevino's been actin' like he's the one graduating all week. Tryin' to rush me to do everything. We went out to eat with Aunt Dawn last night and he was rushin' me. He kept sayin' he had some shit to handle after dinner. I'm nervous and he knows that.

I invited my momma and Bloccc to the graduation, but I don't know if they're coming or not. Over the years, we've see each other here and there but not regularly. I try to go even if it's just for a little while over there every holiday, but with Lil' Vino, lately I haven't even been doing that. My momma or Bloccc didn't hold their tongue tellin' me how dumb I was. My momma calls or texts me at least once a week tellin' me to leave Sevino. That has a lot to do with why our relationship is so fucked up now.

"What 's wrong?" Sevino asked as he drove.

"I'm nervous, Vino, and you already know that," I said, checking my make-up in the mirror.

"For what? Shit, you did the hard part. We finished with that school shit," Sevino suggested.

"We, nigga?"

"Yea, we. Shit, I was up with you while you did homework and still loved you while you were lookin' raggedy doing clinicals. Yeah, muthafuckin' we!" Sevino said, laughing and I muffed him.

We made it to the Denver Coliseum where my graduation is being held. I'm still nervous, and Sevino let me out at the front door, so he could go find a parking spot. I went to grab the door handle, so I could jump out because traffic was behind us, but Sevino stopped me.

"Bitch, go around!" Sevino yelled as he jumped out to open my door.

We kissed briefly, and when I went to walk away, Sevino slapped me on my ass.

"Bitch, you did it!" Black screamed as her and Bloccc and their daughter walked over to where we were standing.

I never understood why Black was so emotional when I had a miscarriage, but I found out a few days later that she was pregnant, and Bloccc was the father.

"Hun, take our picture," Black said, handing her phone to Bloccc.

"Bitch, what the fuck you doin' to him? My brother ain't no picture takin' type of nigga," I whispered.

"Bitch, I'll tell you later," Black yelled in my ear.

"Hoe, I don't want to know." I said, and we smiled for the picture as my momma walked up on us.

Lil' Sevino started whining, so I took him from Sevino with my momma's eyes on me as I soothed Lil' Vino. Bloccc and Sevino didn't even greet each other, but I'm not surprised. This is what they do. Black nor Sevino didn't speak to each other because Sevino can't stand Black, but they usually pretend for me. So, I don't know what the fuck is going on today.

"Congrats, Nikia," Bloccc said as he hugged me, and I kissed his daughter on the cheek that was now in his arms. Then him and Momma walked off.

I'm not surprised that my momma didn't say anything to me. I guess at least I can be grateful that she came. At least she didn't say no foul shit in attempt to bring me down on my day. I don't know if we'll ever be close again, and I'm okay with that. I love Sevino, and I know that he loves me, so until the wheels fall off, I'm rockin' with him.

SEVINO

Watching Shnikia walk across the stage was cool and I know how hard she worked for that shit. I don't want her to work, but I also know that I can't tell her hardheaded ass what to do. When I first met her, she used to go with the flow and didn't say much, but that shit is out the window now. She doesn't give a fuck what she says or when she says it.

"Hun, take our picture," Shnikia said, handing me baby Vino and her phone.

"Man, I ain't ya damn photographer," I spat, trying to pull up the camera as a text message previewed at the top from her momma.

"Take it on Snap," Black threw in.

"Yea, Sevino, take it on Snap," Shnikia threw in as I looked up at her ass while trying to read the text message.

Momma: You're dumb as fuck. Why would you be raising that bitch's baby! I tried to raise you the best that I could, and you still just fucked all that off. Hopefully, one day yo' dumb ass will learn because that nigga is goin' to drag yo' ass through the mud as long as you let him!

I deleted the message as Shnikia whined, telling me to hurry up. I pulled up Snapchat, took a few pictures and handed the phone back to her. If she wants a damn photoshoot, her ass better book one because we not having one today with me taking the fuckin' pictures. Shnikia doesn't need to see that shit.

Fuck that old miserable bitch. I admit that I fucked up, and I shouldn't have been fuckin' with Lay, but I did. She just wants Shnikia to be alone, miserable, and over there with her ass.

I don't have nothin' to do with Lay. Haven't even seen the bitch in years. She called me saying that she had the baby. Shnikia went with me to the hospital, and I was told that she wanted me to take the baby. I don't know why or what the fuck she was goin' through, but she decided that she didn't want my son. So, I did what the fuck I had to do. I didn't know what the fuck I was doin', and I didn't think Shnikia was goin' to step up like she did.

When I told Shnikia what was goin' on, that the bitch left the baby at the hospital and I needed to take him home, she stormed out. I didn't see or talk to Shnikia for two months and then one day, she came home. She talked so much shit, I was ready to put her ass out, but I had to deal with whatever she was going through if I wanted to be with her. I know that she wanted kids and with her condition that wasn't somethin' that could easily happen, so if I wanted her around, I had to deal with the petty shit that she would do. She wouldn't wash a baby bottle, and she would go to the store and get everything under the sun but what the baby needed. It took over a month before she stopped doin' that shit. Then one night I woke up and she was holding the baby in our bed.

My phone started ringing and it's my cousin Trumaine. Considering the fact he's locked up, and I can't call him back, I stepped away to take the call. He got seven years, so he has to do four more years and then he'll be home. I watched Shnikia and as she went through her phone hoping that her ignorant ass momma doesn't send no more text messages tryin' to ruin her day. I talked to Trumaine while Shnikia talked to Black and a few of her classmates.

Baby Vino was falling asleep and I'm ready to put his big ass down. I didn't want to be a dad because of the life that I live.

I'm not leavin' the streets no time soon and I know that with the life I live there is a chance that one day I might not make it home. I don't want to put no kid through that. I never had my parents in my life, and I know how the fuck I felt.

"I'm gon' go out with Black," Shnikia said as she walked up on me, and I ended my call.

"Where?" I asked.

"I don't know. I'm not gon' be gon' that long, and then I'll be home," Shnikia said with an attitude.

"You better have yo' ass home before the club close," I said and she rolled her eyes, kissing me.

I looked over and Black rolled her eyes at me. She just better do what the fuck we discussed.

I MADE my way to the DJ booth with Mailman. Mailman cousin is DJ'ing tonight and he set shit up, so I could do what I needed to do. I had Black bring her here and she went with me last night to pick out the ring. I hate the fuckin' club, but Shnikia loves this shit. I would rather be at the house but not her ass.

"Shout out to all the graduates!" DJ Reck yelled into the microphone as I scanned the crowd for Shnikia and found her and Black sitting in a booth.

I know she sittin' down 'cuz her fuckin' feet hurt. The DJ did the introduction congratulating Shnikia and she finally lifted her head and looked over at the DJ booth as he handed me the mic.

"We done been through some shit, but I ain't startin' over. You rollin' with this West side nigga until the wheels fall off! I want to do this shit forever, so we need to make this shit official, so you can have my last name!" I said into the mic.

Before I could finish, I watched Shnikia take off her heels

and come running towards the DJ booth as I walked down to meet her.

I never seen myself getting married, but I know that is somethin' that Shnikia wanted. It's some shit that she wants that I can't give her no matter how bad I want to. So, I made a promise to myself and her awhile ago that whatever she wanted, no matter what it is, she gon' get. Not on her damn time but mine.

"Will you marry a nigga?" I asked as I dropped down on one knee in front of Shnikia.

"Yes! Yes! Yes!" Shnikia yelled as I stood up, and she wrapped her arms around me tight.

"I love you, Vino," Shnikia said, cryin' into my chest.

"I love you too, Nikia."

THE END

COMING NEXT...